Rocky Rose

This is a work of fiction. The authors have invented the characters. Any resemblance to any persons, living or deceased, is purely coincidental.

Cover Design by Gregory Graphics

Interior Design by Rocky Rose

Edited by Allyson Deese

First RockWrite Publishing Co. trade paperback printing 2017

For more information, or to contact the author, send correspondence to:

RockWrite Publishing

274 Sherman Ave.

New Haven, CT 06511

authorrockyr@gmail.com

Rocky Rose

Acknowledgments

As always, first and foremost, I have to give all praise and thanks to God for He is the one who blessed me with this talent to write, He blessed me with my crazy ass life that I write about. Had it not been for Him blessing the world with my presence, I wouldn't be able to bless my readers and supporters with these books, shout out to you God, you're the real MVP!!

To the real life *Tony*, or as I like to call you, *Oldhead* you are an absolute pain in my ass but I can never and will never deny the love that I have for you. You have always and will always hold a special place in my heart as you have blessed me with the two wonderful gifts a person could give, my babies. We don't always get along; we don't always agree but one thing neither of us can deny is the love we have for one another. I love you with my whole heart, and I thank you for always supporting me, even when I irk your nerves!

Chandrea, words can never fully express how grateful I am to you for the friend and confidant you have been to me over the years. You have always been a straight shooter when it comes to telling me about myself and for that, I'm eternally grateful, not too many people have the gall to do that, I thank you for being who you are. FOE *Family Over Everything!!

Allison Grace, where do I begin baby mama?! *insider* You inspire me to go harder and do better, I love the way our Facebook relationship blossomed into a sisterly bond. No words can ever express my gratitude to you for who you are in my life. I thank you from the bottom of my heart for everything you've done for me from our talks to your advice, I love you sis.

My big brother Yay, where the hell do I begin? Let's see, from the moment we met and formed this brother/sister bond you've been supportive of me, more supportive than a certain person I was dealing with at the time whom shall remain nameless. You not only supported both of my books but when you were locked up, you had others supporting me as well! That's real love and support right there and I'm so grateful to you for it. When you came home, you had people supporting me, family and friends alike, you don't know how that makes me feel!! Thank you for always keeping it a buck with me, despite how I got *kicked out* of your family, *LMAO*, you still ride for me and you know without a question I still ride for you. When I make it, you know without the shadow of a doubt that you will be amongst those very few who I take to the top with me.

My sister from another mister, Ebony McMillan, I could go on and on about how much you mean to me, but I think that would be longer than this novel lol. You are such a great mother, friend, confidant, and help to me and those around you. You are a rare gem to authors like myself and you offer your help selflessly. You have become not only a friend but also family to me.

Lastly, I would be remiss if I didn't thank all of my supporters, for without all of you, there would be no me!! The outpour of love shown to me with my first novella, I Win You Lose, and then with my debut novel, My Man My Abuser, I am eternally grateful for your love and support and just know that this is only the beginning!!

If I forgot to mention anyone who has helped me along this journey of completing this novel, which was supposed to be released in 2014, I do apologize, charge it to my head, not my heart, I love you all, I wouldn't be who I am today had it not been for y'all!!

Now, please, sit back, relax, grab a drink and prepare to enjoy this ride Qortni and Tony are about to put you on!!

Always nothing but love,

Rocky Rose

Rocky Rose

Prologue

Before I was able to respond to Amber, my phone rang, it was Tony.

Before I answered his call I had to compose myself, "Hey sweetie what's going on?"

"Nothing much ma, chilling here, thinking about you. Everything all right with you there? I'm sensing something is wrong."

Tony lived in New Jersey, and when he and I met, he was up here visiting family and his two daughters that lived here. I sometimes took day trips down there to see him and hit up the mall.

"Everything is cool, I'm at my cousins' house right now, she and I are about to go out for a little while."

"Qort, something isn't right, I can hear it all in your voice, now be real with me, what's going on?"

I began crying, I don't know what it was about Tony but he could always sense when something wasn't right with me, even if I was on the phone with him, I could never hide my emotions from him.

I began crying and said, "Qamar and I had a huge fight, he dragged me down the street with his car and I went and whooped his ass, now I'm bleeding and I think I may be having a miscarriage but I don't want to go to the hospital right now, I honestly don't want to save this baby, I don't want to be tied to him at all, by no means necessary I just want this nightmare of a relationship to end."

As Tony and I engaged in conversation Amber, and I were in her car on our way to the hospital so I could get checked out, even though we both pretty much already knew what the outcome was.

"Qortni listen to me please, let your cousin take you to the hospital so you can get checked out, the last thing I want to happen to you is for you to be losing too much blood because of the miscarriage, then I want your cousin to come pick me up from the train station, I'm going to pay ole boy a visit, then once you're cleared from the hospital I want you to come to Jersey with me for a few days."

"Tony I need to handle this myself; I don't want you getting caught up in my battles. You're not even supposed to be leaving the state, I don't want you to come up here, do something crazy and land yourself back in jail, I wouldn't feel right having that happen to you. After I get checked out at the hospital and get cleared, I'll come stay with you for a couple of days, retail therapy will be just what I need to get over all of this bullshit."

"I'll be down there this weekend Qort, you're coming back to Jersey with me after that, call me in the morning or after you come from the hospital, either way call me, no matter the time, just call me to let me know you're all right."

"Okay sweetie, I'll call you."

"Sounds like you and Tony are pretty serious."

"No, just good friends, I can talk to him about anything, he's been my shoulder to cry on and listening ear since we've met, he's a really good guy, someone I need in my corner," I responded to her while starting out the car window.

"Good guys and real friends are hard to come by, just make sure he doesn't become a rebound guy

for you, I don't want you getting your heart broken by him, then I'll have to kick his ass."

Once we got to the hospital one of the emergency room technicians wheeled me directly up to the fourth floor of the hospital, the labor and delivery unit. I was then taken into one of the triage rooms where one of the mid-wives on duty came in to check me, and as suspected, I lost the baby the fetus was in me, I had to push it out

After I delivered my still born baby I was taken into a room that I would be staying in for about

another day or so before I was released from the hospital, and after getting settled into my room there was a knock on my door.

"Come in," I told whomever it was knockin' on my room door.

When my door opened, I almost passed out; they were guests I definitely wasn't expecting to see in my room.

"Are you Ms. Qortni Monroe?" the short one asked.

"Yes, is there something I can help you officers with?" I asked with the most perplexed look on my face.

"Ms. Monroe, we have a warrant for your arrest, we need you to get dressed and come down to the police station with us so you can give us your statement about what happened between you and Mr. Daniels tonight."

"Statement? Arrest warrants? Are you kidding me? I just gave birth to a still born baby! And you're coming up in here to arrest me and make me give a statement? He really called the cops on me?!"

"Any and all questions can be answered down at the station ma'am, now can you please get dressed and come with us?"

Amber began crying her eyes out, I was just a bit stunned, I was in too much shock to cry, I couldn't, I was numb to the pain Qamar kept throwing at me. In fact, I thought this whole night was pretty funny, especially him calling the cops on me after he dragged me down the street knowing I was pregnant.

I began getting dressed and I told Amber to call Tony to let him know what was going on and I instructed her to meet me at the courthouse in the morning, thankfully today is Thursday, so there will be no spending the weekend in lock up for me. Good thinking on my part right?

The police officers read me my Miranda rights, cuffed me and once we got outside of the hospital they placed me in the paddy wagon. Once the officers rounded up everyone that was wanted that evening in the paddy wagon we all made our way to the main police station on Union Avenue. Once we got out we were all searched by one of the judicial marshals at the jail and then placed into a cell, and me being me, I gave the female marshal a tough time because she was purposely roughly searching me like she had something against me and I didn't know this woman from a can of paint, long story short, she wasn't the only one who was leaving bruised up, I made sure she felt my wrath.

I didn't bother making my one phone call, I mean it was pointless, no one at my parent's house was going to answer the phone and I know for damn sure no one was going to bail me out, trifling right? Instead of crying like a punk and being mad at Qamar for me being locked up, I started to reflect on my life over the past few years and how I needed to change things quickly before I ended up either doing jail time or in the ground six feet under.

Friday Morning

I couldn't sleep for shit last night I mean how could I? Did they really expect people to sleep in a cold ass cell on metal beds with no cushion, blankets or pillows? Did they really expect me to pee in a cell where there was no privacy, copping a squat in front of the other two hundred or more people in cells around me? I think not, I was up all night reflecting on my life and came to the conclusion that my life and sanity are far more important than being miserable and going through miscarriage after miscarriage with Qamar, so I was officially done with him, there was no looking back, no turning back, I'd be a fool to. Around nine o'clock the marshal's opened up the cells and allowed us to make a couple of phone calls to see if we could get someone to bail us out so we wouldn't have to go to court, but of course, all the phones at my parents house blocked calls from jails, and the only number

I was able to get through to was my aunt's office number, but of course just because I needed her she wasn't in her office, but I guess it didn't matter because I'm pretty sure she didn't have five thousand dollars laying around to bail me out, so off to court I went. After all who wanted to make calls did, the marshal's handcuffed all of our hands and shackled all of our feet together two by two before we got into the van to be transported to the courthouse.

Once we got to the courthouse we were all brought to the basement where they had holding cells so we could wait for our cases to be called or for attorney's or counselor's to come and talk to us, in my case a state counselor for domestic cases came and talked to me, but I really wasn't trying to hear her, I mean not for nothing, I knew I needed to get out of the situation I was in, so her words were going in one ear and out the other with me, that was until she told me that my older brother was in the court room waiting for my case to be called, that's when my ears perked up, my heart started racing and the tears began to freely fall from my eyes.

"Ms. Monroe, why are you crying all of a sudden? Is it something I said?"

"I can't allow my brother to see me like this, my hair is a mess, I'm cuffed at the wrists, my feet are shackled, this is not how I want him to see me, he can't see me like this."

"He's in some type of uniform, what does he do for a living?"

"He's a correction officer for the state, he sees others like this on a daily basis, he can't see his little sister like this, it's just not right."

"You'll be alright, I promise you, since this is your first offense you'll get a PTA and maybe a year of probation, and they'll probably try to get you to go to anger management classes or something, but you won't be doing any jail time, very rarely does that happen to those who are first offenders."

I nodded my head and went back to my holding cell to wait for my case to be called. As I walked into the courtroom I locked eyes with my brother and my heart sank, I felt like I let him down, I felt like a failure, I felt like shit. When I stood up in front of the judge as the marshal ran down my charges I said a silent prayer that he would let me off with a promise to appear and probation, I couldn't go to jail for whooping Qamar's ass, I'm too pretty for jail, I might get turned out, because fucking with Qamar for this long, I actually forgot what good, strong dick felt like.

"Ms. Monroe, I'm going to give you a later date to appear in court, and I would advise you not to miss that court date or there will be a warrant out for your arrest, do you understand me?"

"Yes your honor, I understand."

"Good, now since Mr. Daniels has decided not to press charges on you, I have to ask you if you would like to press charges against him, but before you answer I must warn you that if you do in fact press charges against him the both of you will be facing jail time, now do you wish to press charges against Mr. Daniels?"

"No your Honor, I'll wave all charges that are against him."

"Very well then, you are free to go and you need to be back in court a month from Monday," the judge responded then banged his gavel against the sounding block and had the marshal call the next case.

I was taken to the side of the courtroom where the marshals un-cuffed me and unshackled my feet, then my brother met me outside.

"Qort, dad is on the phone for you," my brother told me.

I took the phone from his hand and promptly pressed the *end* button, my father was one person I wasn't in the mood to be talking to right now. As my brother and I were walking down the stairs of the courthouse waiting for my brother-in-law to circle the block to bring us home, my brother asked me what happened, since he had just found out about it only hours earlier when he was getting off work. I gave him the whole run down of the previous nights' events, and I ended the conversation by telling him that I didn't regret anything I did, if I had to do it all over again I would in a heartbeat.

Once I got home, I was greeted by my aunt, which explained why she hadn't answered her work phone when I tried to call her earlier; anyhow, she embraced me in a hug and asked me if I was all right, I told her I was and then made my way up to where my room was so I could take a warm bath.

As I was running my bath water I put Epsom salt in the water because my joints were aching, very bad move because I totally forgot about all of the bruises I had all over because of the bullshit I endured last night, needless to say, I made that bath a very quick one, then laid down for a couple of hours before I headed to my younger brother's football game.

After about four hours of sleeping my ringing cell phone woke me up, it was my brother in law calling to see if I was driving to the game myself or if I was riding with him and my brother and of course I told him I was riding, I wasn't really in the mood to be behind the wheel, I needed to relax as much.

An hour after the game

When I got home from the game, which in fact my brother's team won, I noticed my personal room phone had fifteen missed calls, some of which were from Quetta, some were from Tony and most of them were from Qamar's aggravating ass. I decided to call Quetta back in the morning, but I was definitely going to return Tony's phone calls, he had a strange way of making me feel as if everything was going to be all right.

"Qortni, are you all right? You had me worried."

"I'm fine Tony, I'm home, I'm good; how are you?"

"I'm better now that I'm on the phone with you, what happened to you? It's not like you to not return my phone calls; did I do or say something to upset you?"

"No you didn't, I got arrested last night, long story, I'll fill you in on everything that happened next time I see you," I told him not really wanting to have to explain again the events of last night, I did enough of that already today with too many people.

Tony and I talked for a good two hours on the phone before I decided to call it a night; I was mentally and physically exhausted. Just as I was about to fall into a deep sleep, my house phone rang, and I honestly thought it was Tony calling back to mess with me, so I answered it.

"I thought I told you I was going to call you back in the morning after I got myself together, what? You just had to hear my voice one more time before you went to sleep?

"Why the fuck didn't you answer any of my calls? Where the hell were you?" Do you not remember that you need to check in with me when you go out? What the hell is wrong with you?"

It wasn't Tony on the other line of the phone; it was Qamar, so I calmly responded, "Qamar, you do realize that the events of last night ended out relationship right? We are no longer a couple, we're done and over with! Get it through your head that Qortni and Qamar are no longer a couple! I want and need you to understand that besides the fact that the lives you gave me are the same lives you took away from me; I can't deal with you any longer or I'm going to lose my sanity. I'm happy not being with you, this has not worked for us since we got together, I never checked in with you, you never had me on a rope like that, now please refrain from calling me any longer as I may be inclined to call the cops on your ass this time around," I told him then hung up the phone before he had a chance to respond...

Qortni

I couldn't believe he had the audacity to actually call me like everything was all right; I mean really? What the hell was he thinking? I so wanted to call the cops on that bastard but that wouldn't solve anything, it would only make matters worse, I was going to handle him myself in my own way. I got up out of my bed, picked up my iPod from my dresser, started my slow jams playlist, laid back down and allowed my music to put me to sleep.

~The Next Morning~

I didn't sleep too well last night so I decided to give Tony a call to see if he would like some company for the weekend, I needed to get out of New Haven for a little while and where better to go than New Jersey? I could shop and spend time with Tony and de-stress all in one, if it was only for a few days.

"What's up beautiful, how are you doing?" Tony asked as soon as he answered the phone.

"I'm good sweetie, didn't sleep too well last night, I was wondering if you wanted some

company down there this weekend? I could use some retail therapy and some time away from New Haven."

"I would love that, check the train schedule and let me know what time you'll be getting down here so I can meet you at the station."

"Uh, no, I'm driving down there, so when I'm ready to come back all I have to do is jump in my car and be gone. I'm about to get up, shower, get dressed and pack a few things, I'll call you when I get on the road."

"All right Qort, I'll talk to you in a little while."

After getting off the phone with Tony I decided to call Amberlin to see how she was doing, I hadn't talked to her since the night I had gotten arrested.

"Hey hoe, what's going on with ya? I haven't heard from you in a while."

"Nothing much trick, I was just about to call you, how are you feeling? Have you and Qamar made up yet?"

I was a little irritated by her question, I guess Amber like everyone else thought that him and I were going to get back together just like we do every other time we break up, but that wasn't happening this time around, I was done with Qamar and there was no getting back together with him, that fool tried to kill me.

"No, we haven't made up nor have we gotten back together, that won't be happening, when he tried to kill me two nights ago that was the end of our chapter, there's no resurrecting our relationship."

"So, what's your plans for the weekend?"

"I'm heading down to Jersey for the weekend with Tony, I need to get away from New Haven for a little while."

"I'm going to say this to you then I'm going to leave it alone because I know it's probably going to go in one ear and out the other but listen, don't allow

27

Tony to be your rebound guy, you and Qamar were together for three years, don't go hop in bed with Tony thinking he's going to take whatever hurt away from you that you're experiencing."

"I hear what you're saying but it's not even like that, I mean Tony and I are just friends, we haven't slept together, and neither one of us has made a pass at the other, we're just friends, he's

something like my best male friend, and I don't want to compromise our friendship by adding sex to the equation."

"I hear you cuz, I just don't want you or him getting hurt by each other by rushing into things, that's all I'm saying. I haven't met him yet but I can tell that you really like him, I'm not sure as to how much or on what level but I can tell you really like him, so just be careful."

"I appreciate your concern Amber, I really do now I'm going to have to cut this conversation short because I still need to get up, shower, pack and get on the road, trying to go shopping when I get down there, I freaking love the mall down there."

"Alright chica, call me when you get down there to let me know you made it all right, and if I don't answer, text me or leave a message."

"Alright mama, I'll hit you up later," I responded before ending the call and headed to jump in the shower.

After getting out of the shower and packing, I packed my car up and began my way to New Jersey. Once I hit mid-New York I called Tony to let him know that I was on my way and to get his address.

"How long before you get here mama?" he asked me.

"According to my GPS I should arrive in half an hour."

"Wait, where are you at? You're not just leaving your house are you? There's no way."

"No, I'm already half way through New York, you act like Jersey is a five hour ride from Connecticut," I told him laughing, he obviously didn't know that I was a speed racer when it came to driving, I definitely put the pedal to the metal.

"Well, when you get to my crib, call me and I'll come out, I don't want you getting out of the car, especially because it'll be dark out and I'm not trying to have something happen to you with these

knuckle heads out here."

"All right sweetie, I'll call you when I get there."

Once I got to Tony's place I saw why he didn't want me getting out of the car, there was a bunch of suspect looking guys hanging out in front of the main entrance to his apartment building. I stood outside right next to my car, not even closing the car door to stretch my legs and to call him to let him know I was outside, boy was that the wrong move to make, I think out of the ten guys that were standing in front of the building about eight of them tried to talk to me, but Tony killed all of that noise when he came outside.

He pulled me in for a hug, and whispered in my ear; "You trying to have a dude out here fighting over you? I told you to stay in the car when you got here, did you think these dudes wouldn't be checking for you?"

I whispered back, "Let them check, I'm single now, so they can look all they want; let me find out you're jealous?"

He smacked me on my ass and replied, "You won't be single too much longer, now let's go, my brother-in-law is letting us use his crib for the weekend."

Tony and I spent Friday night and Saturday morning locked up in his brother-in-law's house

Saturday afternoon we went shopping at the Jersey Gardens Mall then grabbed a bite to eat.

"Qort, when are you going back to CT?"

"Probably tomorrow afternoon so I can get ready for work on Monday, why what's up?"

"What if we go back now and you can stay with me at my brother's crib? He's closer to your job than your house."

"We? You going to CT?"

"Yeah, got some things to handle and I have to go see my daughters, you down?"

"You're driving, I'm tired, someone kept me up all night last night," I told him with a smirk on my face.

"I can handle that; do you want to come with me to see my daughters?"

"Nah, I'm good, your baby mothers may not be cool with me being around so I'm going to probably stop by my grandmother's house while you handle your business."

"They won't have a problem but I respect your decision, I'll drop myself off and when I'm done I'll just call you to come get me.

"Sounds like a plan," I told him as we cleared our table and headed to my car.

Tony

T here was something about Qortni the day we met in the hospital that instantly attracted me to her and I still to this day don't know what it is.

She's not like any of the other females I've encountered or deal with, she's younger but she definitely has her head on her shoulders, she's determined and she had her future mapped out already, she's definitely someone I need on my team.

In such a short period of time things between her and I have been moving rather quickly, but I'm content with it, but I must take into consideration her feelings because she just got out of a very fucked up relationship with her punk ass ex Qamar. I've never met the dude but I could always tell that Qortni was too good for him, but I could never tell Qortni that because I didn't want her to think I was throwing shade on her relationship with him, that's not my style.

While we were at lunch and I asked her to stay with me when we got back to Connecticut I honestly didn't think she would agree but to my surprise she did. I love spending time with her even though she acts as if she's not really interested in me, I know it's all an act; she's not fooling no one but herself.

After getting back in Connecticut I dropped myself off at my oldest daughter's mothers house and told Qortni that I'd either call or text her when I was done handling what I needed to handle.

Qortni

Spending the weekend with Tony had me in my feelings, like I really do like him but I don't want to move too fast, especially being that I just out of that long term relationship with Satan himself, I mean Qamar. I should have told Tony that I was going back to my house for the remainder of the weekend but I love being in his presence. Plus, I'm not really ready to deal with the stress that comes with staying at my house.

After Tony dropped himself off at his oldest daughter's mother's house I went over to my grandmother's house to spend some time with her since it's been a while since I'd been over there.

Tony

Later that Evening...

My oldest daughter's mother Angel caught a major attitude with me when she saw Qort in the car when I went over to her house earlier and when Qort picked me up, she's salty 'cause things between us will never be the same as they were back when we were together. I won't lie, I do break her off sometimes when I'm in town but it's only to shut her whining ass up, after a while that shit gets annoying so I give her the dick to keep her from constantly complaining and it works every time. After about two hours of spending time with both of my daughters I called Qort to come scoop me so we can go to my brother's crib, I know she has to go to work in the morning and I don't want to hold her up from getting enough sleep tonight.

When we got to my brother's crib I could tell something was bothering her. She asked if she could hop in the shower really quick and I told her yes and that I would join her. Let me just say, that girl got mega talent. After we got out of the shower she still seemed as if something was on her mind. After we got dressed, we headed into the kitchen so I could fix us something to eat and when I did she told me her true feelings for me. I was shocked to say the least 'cause Qortni is not the type to voice her feelings for someone for fear of rejection, she's told me that on numerous occasions. Even though she didn't come right out and say that she loved me, she did tell me that she has fallen hard for me and I can't front, I'm feeling the same way about her.

Can I be honest with y'all for a second? Do I love Qortni? I can honestly say that I do but it's going to take me a very long time before I admit it to her, if I ever admit it to her. You see I'm not one to openly share my emotions with females I really have strong feelings for. Which is why I can honestly say my previous relationships never really worked out. I wonder if Qort is the one female that could help me get over my bad habit.

Qortni broke me out of my thoughts when she said, "I thank you for understanding Tony, I really do but I honestly think we're too far along in this 'thing' of ours for me to just decide now to slow things down, it'll make things a lot more complicated," avoiding eye contact with me so I wouldn't see the tears rolling down her face.

"No need to thank me Ma, I want to do whatever I can to make you most comfortable and if that means slowing things down, then so be it, I'm rockin' with you Shorty. I think you're right though, I think we are too far along in what we have going on to just start falling back from one another."

"Let me ask you a serious question and I would really appreciate an honest answer."

"Shoot."

"What are we doing with one another? I'm not interested in having a fuck buddy, and my feelings for you are way too strong for us to be just friends."
"Honestly Qort, I don't know what to make of or call what we're doing, I mean I don't want you to feel as if we have to rush into a relationship with one another because you need time to heal from you precious relationship."

"Thank you for your honesty," she said heading back into the bedroom.

I said following her, "You're not upset with me are you? If we do end up in a relationship I want you to totally have that punk Qamar out of your system and I want to have you fully to myself, mind, body and soul."

"Why would I be mad or upset with you for being honest with me? I have no choice but to respect your honesty and take it for what it is," she told me before putting her last forkful of food in her mouth.

"Cool, so what time do you have to be at work in the morning?"

"Seven thirty and I get off at four."

"Do you mind dropping me off on Howard Ave in the morning?"

"I can do that, you cooking me breakfast in the morning?"

"I got you Ma but I'm telling you now, I don't eat pork so I won't be cooking you any, you gonna have to get that elsewhere."

"No problem, I can get that from work, I just want breakfast before I go in."

"Cool, you up for watching a movie with me until we doze off?"

"Absolutely, what movie do you have in mind?" she asked while heading into the kitchen to fix another plate.

"American Gangster with Denzel Washington, have you seen it yet?"

"No, matter of fact, wasn't that the movie we were supposed to be going to see but you were taking too long that night so I bounced?"

"Yea, I think you're right; bring me two wine coolers when you come back in please, I'm going to start the movie and change the sheets on the bed."

Qortni

I'm glad I told Tony my feelings for him but what I neglected to tell him was that I was really falling in love with him in just these past few months, I figured that would be a bit much, I didn't want to run him away, that would certainly break my heart.

Tony and I decided to watch a movie after we both ate, I fixed another plate, grabbed him and I a few wine coolers and headed back into the bedroom. I wanted to ask him whose house he was going to at seven in the morning but technically it was none of my business so I left well enough alone, I wasn't trying to start an argument with him tonight 'cause it would only lead to me going back to my house and being mad at myself for starting some shit.

As soon as I got comfortable on the bed and started on my second plate my phone started singing Eve's song You Had Me You Lost Me letting me know it was Qamar calling me and like an idiot I answered, Tony excused himself to give me some privacy.

"How can I help you Qamar?" I asked with a major attitude.

"How are you Qortni? You have been on my mind for some time now and I wanted to know if it's possible for you and I to talk and possible work on getting back together and try to rebuild and repair our relationship?"

"Qamar, do me a favor and listen to me closely and hear what I'm telling you, we will never, ever get back together, you tried to kill me not too long ago and now you expect me to have a civilized conversation with you and you think there's a chance in hell for us to rebuild and repair a relationship that's too far beyond repair? Our relationship didn't mean a thing to you from the beginning so why try to make things better now? It's too late to try to rebuild anything between you and I, now please don't ever call my phone again, I would greatly appreciate it," I told him before handing up on him before he had a chance to get another word in.

Tony walked back in the room shaking his head.

"What are you shaking your head for?"

"You and old boy, you just dumbed out on him, you good?"

"I've never been better, he's attempting to repair something that's beyond repair, I can't and won't allow myself to go down that road with him again. He's never respected our relationship or me so there's no point in trying to rebuild something that wasn't healthy to begin with. I'm over him and what I thought was a relationship."

He walked over to the bed, pulled me up, hugged me and told me, "One day he's going to realize what he had in you and he's going to kick himself in the ass for fucking up what he had with you. You're now an average type of chick Ma, and he doesn't yet realize that. I mean you and I have known each other for a little while and I can already tell that you're a different type of woman from most of the women in New Haven; don't stress over him and what y'all used to have, focus on what you want for the future and your happiness."

I could do nothing but smile and hug him. We both got comfortable in the bed, drank our wine coolers and started to watch the movie, before I started kissing him all over, and well, you know what that lead to.

I planted small kisses on his face and worked my way down to his chest, when I got to his nipples I circled each one of them with my wet tongue, he moaned in pleasure and I felt his manhood begin to rise, I guess he was enjoying what I was doing to him. I allowed my tongue to continue its journey further south until I reached his manhood. I kissed his dick through his boxers, enjoying myself with each kiss, I slipped his manhood out of the slit in his boxers and planted soft, wet kisses all over it, I couldn't tell who was getting more aroused, him or I.

After gently teasing him with small sensual kisses, I placed his already hard dick into my mouth and he groaned out in pure ecstasy. I started sucking his penis nice and slow, then I picked up my pace and before I knew it he was matching my rhythm with thrusts of his own, my personal goal was to get him to cum from head since he said he's never been able to before. I was into my groove pleasing Tony with head and before I knew it he had flipped me over on my back, tore my brand new Victoria's Secret panties off of me and wasted no time in feasting on my love box, he was eating me out like I was the best meal he ever partook of.

I must have cum three or four times from his heavenly tongue and when he was about to start again, all I could manage to say was, "fuck me."

He obliged my request with no words, just actions and when he entered me all I could do was gasp because of his width, it got me every time. He started with slow strokes and wet kisses on my neck, then moved to my chest where he took turns putting each one of my breasts into his warm mouth and sucked on them like he was a newborn baby seeking nourishment.

I loved the sexual chemistry Tony and I shared, it was like no other. He took his time sexing my body, it wasn't a marathon for him, seeing who could finish first, he took the time to learn my body what turned me on and what turned me off. An hour went by when we both climaxed at the same time. He collapsed right beside me breathing heavily and so was I. Once I was able to get up I went to the bathroom, cleaned myself up and then went to the bedroom to clean him up.

"Qort, you do know I'm capable of washing myself up right?"

"I know but you put in work, this is the least I could do for you."

"I respect it; I have to tell you though, you are the only one out of all of the women I've ever dealt with that actually cleaned me up after we've had sex, that says a lot about you, in my book."

"It's nothing, now start the movie over please and I promise to be on my best behavior this time around," I told him smiling.

He started the movie over, I laid on his chest and we watched it until it was watching us.

The next morning, we both overslept which meant we didn't have time for breakfast, we jumped in the shower quickly, squeezed in a quickie and headed out the door. I was lucky 'cause where he needed to be dropped off at was literally down the block from my job, I clocked in, just in the nick of time.

Tony

Qortni was a different type of woman, not like any of the chicks I was used to dealing with. After we talked, and she expressed her feelings towards me I started to feel like shit, I knew what I was doing was wrong but, I honestly didn't think my feeling towards her would escalate the way they did. You see, after I got out of federal prison I reconnected with the chick I had been dealing with since before I moved to Jersey. We have history, years together. I don't want to hurt her, and I definitely don't want to hurt Qortni, I guess I'm just going to have to play both sides of the fence until I get caught. The only question is, who will I want to be with if or when that day comes?

When Qortni dropped me off I gave her a kiss and went into Diane's house, unbeknownst to me, Diane was watching me through the window the whole time.

"So is she the reason you decided to stay at your brother's house since you came back in town?"

"It's too early for your bullshit Diane, I'm tired and all I want to do is go to sleep for a couple of hours."

"Fuck you Tony."

"Why all of this so early in the morning? Did I say I was fucking her? No I didn't, she's a friend of mine and since Jace couldn't give me a ride over here I called her to give me a ride since I knew she had to work, calm down with all of the unnecessary drama."

"Tony, you better not be lying to me, that's all I have to say. Let's get a quickie in before I have to go to work," she told me tugging at my jeans.

Honestly I really wasn't in the mood to have sex with Diane, sexing Qort last night and this morning had me spent, hopefully this quickie was quicker than usual so I can take my ass to bed, being tired was an understatement.

"I got you Ma, pull your jeans down," I told her while taking my dick out of my jeans and turning her around; I wasn't even in the mood for foreplay and I think she noticed it.

I sexed her quickly so she could be on her merry way to work and so I could jump in the shower and get some sleep. After my shower I got something to eat, turned on EPSN and text Qortni. We text back and forth until my eyes closed.

"Hey Ma, just hitting you up to let you know I have you on my mind."

"Hey sweetie, I'm flattered, you got me blushing at work. How's your morning going so far for you?"

"It's cool, nothing exciting going on in my world, just hopped out of the shower, bout to shut it down for a couple of hours, someone kept me busy last night."

"My kitty is sore and a bit swollen thanks to a certain somebody. I can't wait to get off, take a shower and go to bed, I feel as if I had a great workout last night, LOL," she text me back.

I text back, "Am I going to see you later this evening?"

"It's definitely a possibility…matter of fact, yes 'cause I left my bag at your brother's house, I didn't think to grab it this morning."

"Bet, well I'm about to shut it down. If I don't text you before you get off hit my jack when you're about to leave work."

"Alright sweetie, talk to you later."

I turned the bedroom television on to ESPN, caught up on all of the sports news until I fell asleep.

I must have been sleep for about five hours, it didn't even seem that long, my ringing phone woke me, and it was my brother Jace.

"What's good bruh?"

"Ain't shit, you still at my crib?"

"Nah, I had Qort drop me off at Diane's house this morning, what's up?"

"I need you to skate to New York with me real quick, I have to meet up with a couple of people, it's only going to take me about half an hour to do what I need to do, you can drive back home."

"Aight, come scoop me, all I have to do is get dressed, I'll be ready by time you get here."

"Aight."

I really didn't want to take that ride with my brother but I knew this was business, and business meant money and I never turn down money.

I sent Qortni a text to let her know I was going to be unavailable for a little while and that I'd hit her phone up when I finished handling my business, she responded, "okay."

Qortni

The night I spent with Tony was the most relaxing night I've had in years, it was even better than the night we shared in Jersey, and it was definitely better than any night in the three years Qamar and I spent together.

The sex we had was amazing and his company was even better, I could be myself around him, nothing was forced, meaning my feelings for him were all genuine.

Spending the evening with Tony was a real good look, it definitely made my workday go by smoothly and the fact that he text me to let me know he had been thinking about me made me feel just a little special.

I was a bit upset when he sent me a text telling me that he was going to be unavailable for a little while. For some reason a twinge of jealousy came over me, I almost felt as if he was unavailable because of another female; but I had to check myself because he wasn't my man, and we were not committed to one another.

After leaving work I went home, took a shower then headed over to my cousin's house, I hadn't seen nor talked to her in a while, she was sitting on her front porch when I pulled up.

"Hey hoe, long time no see, what you been up to?"

"Nothing much trick, I've just been working and chilling with Tony, how have you been? I know it's been a while since we spoke.

"I hear that, when am I going to finally meet Tony? You've been keeping him a secret for some time now. How long have y'all known each other now?"

"Well, you know we met like a month and change before all that bullshit between Qamar and I went down, and I haven't been keeping him a secret, I'm just in no rush for him to meet the family, you know I'm a pretty private person."

"I hear ya, I'm about to get dinner started, you staying?"

"Yeah, um, what's going on with you and Nathan? I haven't seen him in a while, when's the wedding?"

"The wedding will be the end of this year, I hope you know you're going to be my maid of honor, shoot, maybe you can bring Tony as your date."

"You think you're slick, Tony will not be my date! I'm rolling dolo to the wedding, have you picked out your colors and everything? Wait; has Nathan chose who his groomsmen will be? I'm absolutely not walking down the aisle with Qamar."

"I honestly don't think Qamar will be at the wedding let alone in the wedding, him and Nathan aren't really close anymore, a whole bunch of mess went down with the both of them and Nathan decided to separate himself from Qamar, they haven't spoken in about four months. "

"Damn, I didn't know all of that happened, well then again how would I, Qamar and I don't speak anymore. You have any wine or wine coolers in the house? Think we need to have a girl's night in tonight and do some serious catching up; I've been out of the loop for a while."

"You may need to go to the package store, Nathan and I went through the rest of the wine a few nights ago."

"Nasty asses," I replied on my way to the p.k. at the corner of the block.

When I got back in the house Amber was just putting her homemade rolls into the oven, the rice, black eyes peas, greens and apple pie she made had my stomach doing flips, I hadn't eaten since breakfast this morning. I popped open one of the wine cooler, grabbed a glass from her cabinet and sat at the table.

"So, when are you and Nathan going to try for another baby? Or are you going to wait a few years?"

"We've been talking about it, we've been working on it, I guess it'll happen when it's supposed to happen, we're just enjoying one another right now."

"I hear that, I'm so happy for the both of you, I swear when you and Nate broke up a few years back I really didn't think you'd end up back together, that was a rough break."

"Had it not been for you and Qamar dating, Nate and I probably wouldn't have gotten back together, so we have you to thank for us getting back together. Tell me more about mysterious Tony; have you met his family yet? What are they like? Does he have kids?"

"Slow down! He's such a sweetheart, he's a real cool, chill type of guy, I met his brother, he has two daughters, they're like six months apart I think, haven't met them yet, haven't met anyone else in his family yet either. I really like him, such a difference between him and Qamar, like I can be myself around him; my feelings for him aren't strained, and the sex is just indescribable!"

"Wait, two daughters six months apart? Seriously? Have you met their mothers?"

"Nah, he wanted me to the other day but I told him they probably wouldn't be comfortable with meeting me or having me around their children. I have to admit though, I'm feeling like he has another female that he's messing with and even though technically I can't be mad 'cause we're not in a relationship, I do have really strong feelings for him and I can't shake them as much as I would like to."

"Ask him. When you talk to him again ask him if he has a girlfriend."

"I can't do that; I'll be totally overstepping my bounds."

"Well you don't really want to know if he has a girl or not," Amber told me as she started fixing my plate.

"I do want to know but I don't want to overstep my bounds, what if I piss him off?"

"Oh well, your feelings are way more important than his, I don't want to see you hurt again or in another situation similar to the one you were in with Qamar, I don't want to have to whoop his ass if he hurts you."

"You ain't fighting no one, I'm going to ask him this evening, I'm supposed to see him after he gets back in town."

"Just brace yourself for whatever his answer may be, I honestly don't want to see you get hurt, I know you have very strong feelings for him, just by the way your face lights up every time his name is mentioned."

Just as I was about to put another forkful of food in my mouth, my phone rang.

"Speaking of him," I said to Amber as I excused myself from the kitchen to take the call.

"Hello."

"What's up gorgeous?"

"Nothing much, at my cousin's house eating and drinking, what's up with you?"

"Nothing much Ma, just getting back in town with my brother, am I still going to see you tonight?"

"Yea, after I bounce from my cousin's house I'll see you."

"Aight' you can come right to my brother's house, I'll be there with him and his boy."

"Alright."

"You alright? You sound as if something is bothering you."

"I'll talk to you about it when I see you, it's not really a conversation I want to have over the phone."

"Okay, well, I'll see you when you get here."

I hung up with Tony and went back into the kitchen to fix another plate of food and pour myself another drink.

"Everything alright with you?"

"Yea, I'm good, just trying to mentally prepare for this conversation with Tony, you know a women's intuition never fails her, and my gut is telling me that he's dealing with someone else."

"Well, drink up, I'm sure you're going to need to be pretty buzzed when you approach him on it."

"You're right about that."

After another plate of food, three more wine coolers and two more hours of catching up with my cousin I decided it was time to bounce, I needed to confront Tony while I was still buzzed and had the guts to do so.

When I got to Jace's house Tony was outside smoking and on the phone, I almost felt bad for whomever was on the other end of the conversation with him 'cause he was damn sure barkin' on them, to be honest, it was kind of comical to me.

I killed the ignition on my car, grabbed my plate of food and told Tony I'd meet him inside the house, he nodded and continued on with his conversation. When I got into the house I greeted Jace and his roommate who went by the nickname Swag; I don't who gave him that nickname and why, but, whatever.

Swag asked me if I smoked and I told him yes, I never turn down free weed. I took a few tokes off of it before Tony motioned for me to join him in the front room so I obliged, he didn't smoke weed, mainly because he had to keep his urine clean for his weekly visits to his probation officer.

"What's up Ma? Sorry to keep you waiting, one of my baby mothers kept pissing me off so I had to set her ass straight, how was your day?"

"It was cool except for the fact that my kitty was sore and swollen. How was your day? Did you handle the business you needed to handle? Do you have a girlfriend?"

"Whoa, where did that come from?"

"Just want to make sure I'm not some side piece for you, not trying to get my feelings hurt by another dude, that's all."

"You are the only female I'm checking for, I have absolutely no intentions on hurting you, I have true feelings for you, last thing I want to do is hurt you."

"Cool," I replied. As much as I wanted to believe him, I still had the gut feeling he wasn't being totally honest with me, it felt like he was a professional liar, I wonder if he was a graduate of Bullshit University, I guess only time will tell.

I think he could tell I wasn't totally pleased with his answer but he didn't push the issue, he totally changed the subject on me.

"What do you have planned for the rest of the evening?"

"Nothing really, probably go home and write, got some things I need to get off of my heart and mind, I haven't written in a while."

"How about we go catch a movie, my treat?"

"That's fine, what movie did you have in mind?"

"How about This Christmas with Chris Brown, looks like it's pretty good."

"I'm game, what time does the next movie start?" I asked walking into the kitchen to grab a wine cooler out of the fridge.

"Next movie starts at nine-fifteen, we can leave now if you like, I know how you like to eat so you'll probably want something from the concession stand."

"Shut up and let's go."

"I'm driving so toss me your keys."

I threw my keys to him while walking outside to the car.

Knowing the both of us the movie was the last thing on our minds, now don't get me wrong, I really did want to see this movie, but I was also feigning for sex, all those wine coolers I had at my cousin's house and the one I drank on my way to the movie theater had me feeling some type of way.

When the movie started we watched the first half hour of it then we began to kiss and the kissing let to feeling each other up, and that led to me taking his manhood out of his pants and blessing it with my warm mouth until he was rock hard.

Luckily for us we were sitting in the very back of the theater and no one else was seated back there so I pulled my jeans down and mounted him; still having to get used to his width, I exhaled and began to ride him reverse cowgirl.

Tony had to tell me a few times to lower my voice, my moans were getting to be pretty noisy, but I could help myself, his sex game was on point, the best I had so far.

About twenty minutes into our sex session Tony and I climaxed together and of course he released inside of me, very irresponsible of me, I know, I just prayed I wasn't ovulating then and I didn't end up pregnant.

We watched the rest of the movie without any more sexual interruptions and then he whispered in my ear, "Round two is on when we get home, I'm going to really tear that pussy up."

"Oh, is that right? Who said I wanted there to be a round two? What if our movie rendezvous was good enough for me?" I asked him with a smirk on my face.

He looked at me with a straight face and said, "Now you know damn well that quickie wasn't enough for either of us, so cut the shit."

I laughed and said, "I know, I just wanted to see what you were going to say, now be quiet so we can watch the rest of the movie," then kissed him on his cheek. We watched the rest of the movie, on our best behavior.

When we got back to his brother's house we had to make sure the house was empty before we started sexually attacking one another and once we were sure we were alone, it was on. We undressed one another, our clothes got thrown all around, and before I could blink twice, Tony had picked me up and entered me while holding me, that shit felt so good! I don't even know how much time had lapsed but I definitely enjoyed the whole evening with Tony. After our sexcapade I went into the bathroom to take a shower, I definitely needed it after our evening of intense sex.

Tony

It seems as if every time Qortni and I had sex I was falling for her even more. The sex in the theater blew my mind, I honestly didn't expect her to pull my dick out and top me off, then ride me right there in the back of the theater, she definitely shocked me, but trust, I damn sure wasn't complaining. Being that I didn't want Qortni to think she outdid me at the movies, I made sure I took full control when we got back to the crib and trust, I put in work on her pussy, I am never one to be outdone when it comes to sex.

When Qortni went to take her shower I went to the kitchen to fix me a plate of food, all of that sex had me work up an appetite; after heating up my food I went back into the room, sat on the bed and reached for the remote to turn the television on, as I was reaching for the remote I noticed Qort's phone ringing and from the sound of Eve's song You Had Me You Lost Me being her ringtone I already knew it was her punk ass ex-boyfriend Qamar, so me being me, I answered her phone, "hello?"

"Hello? Um, I may have dialed the wrong number.

"Who were you trying to contact?"

"Qortni Monroe, but I obviously have the wrong number, sorry to interrupt you man."

"Nah, you have the right number, I'm just trying to figure out why you're calling her, and didn't y'all break up?"

"Yeah we did but I need to speak to her, I'm not sure as to who you are but if she's available can you please hand her the phone?"

"She's not available but I will tell her you called and it's none of your concern as to who I am, but I'm telling you now, she's not going to want to speak with you," I told him then hung up without allowing him to say another word.

When Qortni came out of the bathroom into the bedroom only wrapped in a towel, I had to control myself, I wanted to take her right then and there but I refrained from doing so.

"Hey, ya boy Qamar called while you were in the shower, I answered and told him I would tell you that he called," I was expecting her to spazz on me for answering her phone but instead she rolled her eyes and said, "Did he say what he wanted? I really need to change my number; I think I'm going to do that first thing tomorrow morning."

"Nah, he was trying to figure out who I was and said that he needed to speak to you."

"I'm not even going to bother to call him back, I don't want to even know what he wanted to talk to me about, matter of fact, I'm changing my number right now," she said reaching for her phone.

Seeing Qortni cop an attitude for some reason turned me on a little bit, I swear I don't know what it is about her and her personality that drives me crazy.

While I was eating Qortni was on the phone with her phone carrier so she could change her number, I know changing her number was the last thing she wanted to do because of the number of contacts she has in her phone but because Qamar didn't get the memo that she didn't want to be bothered anymore she had to do what was best for her and her peace of mind. Once she finally got off the phone she dropped her towel oiled herself up with baby oil gel, put a tank top on and a pair of female boxers.

"Damn, someone is pretty comfortable around me now," I told her with a wink.

"Why wouldn't I be? I mean me getting dressed or even undressed in front of you is nothing; it's not like you haven't seen me naked before."

"True, but some females still feel shy in front of men they've slept with for some reason, but I can see that you're not one of them."

"Definitely not," she replied.

I know Thanksgiving is coming up and I know things between Qortni and I were escalating but I didn't know if she had holiday plans already set or if she was waiting for me to extend an invitation to her to join me and my family for Thanksgiving dinner in Jersey…

Qortni

Qamar calling me was quite aggravating to say the least, simply because him and I are no longer together and he shouldn't have anything he needs to talk to me about.

What caught me off guard and surprised was the fact that Tony felt very comfortable answering my phone, but it didn't bother me, in all actuality I'm kind of glad he answered when Qamar called, just so Qamar could see for himself that I have moved on and that I had no second thoughts on not being with him anymore.

When I was on the phone getting my number changed I kept feeling Tony's eyes on me and if I said it wasn't turning me on knowing that me in nothing but a towel was turning him on, I'd be lying.

After handling my business on the phone and successfully changing my number and getting dressed I headed in the kitchen to make me a plate from the food Tony and I had the other night; as my plate was heating up I contemplated asking Tony about his plans for Thanksgiving since it was only like two weeks away. I know Thanksgiving morning I'll be at the Elm City Classic football game, Hillhouse vs. Cross but I had no concrete plans for Thanksgiving dinner; I honestly wanted to spend the holiday with him and his family but I didn't want to bring it up, I didn't want to seem pushy, I decided to wait a few more days before I brought it up to him.

When I got back into the room Tony had just started the movie Love Jones.

"Do you like this movie?"

"One of my all time favorites," I responded before placing another forkful of food in my mouth.

"I got great taste then," he said with a smile on his face.

"Whatever punk," I teased with a playful punch to his arm.

We both finished eating, he killed the lights, I laid my head on his chest and he wrapped his right

arm around me and we watched the movie on our best behavior, until the first sex scene came on.

We started out with small sensual kisses, those kisses led to me kissing his chest and from his chest my tongue traveled down to his navel and from there I took had penis out of his pajamas and placed it into my warm, wet mouth. I don't know what it is about giving Tony head that excited me and made me extra wet, whatever it was though, it worked every time.

Tony could do nothing but moan in pleasure and thrust his groin upward to push his dick further in my mouth, we were both in sync; after giving him head I mounted him, against his will because he desperately wanted to taste me, but my mind was on busting a couple of nuts and getting Tony to do the same.

I didn't realize how turned on Tony had me until I squirted all over him and the bed, that was one of the best feelings in the world, something I had never done with Qamar. We went on sexing each other for about an hour and a half before we climaxed together. I had to wait a good fifteen minutes before I could get the strength to get up and shower, I really had a feeling that I wouldn't make it into work in the morning, but I really didn't care, I was on casual status so any extra days I picked up were on my own terms.

After getting out of the shower I grabbed Tony's washcloth, wet it, lathered it up with soap and was on my way back into the bedroom to see if he wanted to freshen up or if he was going to take a shower but I stopped short of the room when I heard Tony on the phone and by the tone of his voice I could tell he was on the phone with a female.

"Listen, I'll be back around tomorrow morning, I have to help my brother handle some things so I'm staying at his crib again tonight, stop bitchin' you'll see me tomorrow."

I knew for sure after hearing him say that he was talking to a female and I wanted to approach him on it but I'd be overstepping my bounds since we weren't technically a couple, I didn't have a real reason to be upset with him or even cop an attitude with him, except for the fact that he lied to me.

While he was still on the phone with the unidentified female I walked in the room as if I didn't hear part of his conversation. He told the person he'd see them tomorrow and ended the call.

"Here's your washcloth, I didn't know if you wanted to use it or if you were going to take a shower," I told him with much attitude, throwing his washcloth at him.

"I'm going to take a shower; did I do something to piss you off? I'm sensing some attitude from you and I'm not feeling it," he asked me.

"I'm good," I told him while beginning to oil my body and get ready for bed, the way I was feeling I already knew I wasn't going into work in the morning.

"Qort, I know you're not good, now tell me what's wrong."

"I said I'm good now can we drop it?"

"Fine, I'm going to take my shower."

"Good for you."

He went into the bathroom without saying another word.

My feelings were really bruised just thinking that Tony either had a girlfriend or was dealing with someone else. While he was in the shower I took the time to call my job to let them know that I wouldn't be in for the morning shift. Being that I wasn't really in the mood to have a conversation or even be bothered by him for the remainder of the evening I decided to listen to some music on my iPod and just write from my heart, I had a ton of emotions that I needed to release. I guess Tony knew that I wasn't in the mood to be bothered because after he got out of the shower he got dressed, laid in the bed and didn't attempt to say anything else to me for the remainder of the evening.

The next morning...

I fell asleep with my iPod still playing when I woke up. Tony wasn't in the bed but I smelled some heavenly food coming from the kitchen but I really didn't feel like being bothered by him still so I went into the bathroom, took a quick shower, got dressed, packed my bag and then went into the kitchen to see if my plate from Amber's house was still in the fridge so I could eat.

"Good morning beautiful," Tony greeted me when I walked into the kitchen.

"Hey."

"What time do you have to be to work today?"

"I called out."

"You feeling alright?"

"Yeah, just don't feel like being bothered today…I think I'm going to treat myself to a shopping spree in Jersey, I'm in the mood to shop."

"Would you like some company? I can drive you there and back."

"Not really in the mood for your company, I just want to vibe out to my music while I cruise down 95-South."

I guess he didn't like the vibe he was getting from me because he turned the stove off and pulled me into his chest, his cologne was making me weak but I didn't want him to know it.

"Qort something isn't right with you and I've noticed it since last night after you got out of the shower, now tell me what's going on with you and I'm not letting you go until you do."

Since I knew he mean what he said, I knew this was the only way for him to leave me be, I

broke down and asked him right out, "Do you have a girlfriend?"

"No I don't," he told me looking directly in my eyes.

"Okay, fine," I replied not believing him and even more pissed that he had the audacity to lie to me right in my face.

"So now that we cleared the air would you like some company to Jersey? I've never known you to pass up a free ride, now let's get dressed and go."

Tony did know me well enough to know that I never turned down an invitation to ride instead of drive so we got dressed and headed out the door. When we got outside before getting in the car Tony lit a bogie and I asked him if he needed to call his home girl and let her know that instead of seeing her this morning the would see her later this evening.

"Qort, what are you talking about?"

"Your female friend you were on the phone with last night when I was getting out of the shower, I mean unless you go both ways and were talking to a guy when you told them to stop bitching and that they would see them tomorrow morning."

He looked defeated, like his secret had been found out.

"We'll talk while we're on the road," he told me taking one last pull on his bogie before flicking it to the ground.

"Whatever," I told him getting into my car. One thing about me is that my intuition never fails me, I don't know why Tony thinks I believe his bullshit, yes I am ten years younger than him in numbers but mentally, I really think I'm ten years older than him.

"Listen Qort, I haven't been completely honest with you since we've met, I do have a girl, her and I have been together on and off for the past ten years, she rode my bid out with me. You know the house you dropped me off to on Congress? That's her house, she knows about you but she only knows you as being a friend of mine, nothing more, nothing less, and for the record, no, I don't go both ways.

I looked at him and simply said, "Cool."

I was numb to the hurt my heart had just endured, some part of me felt as if I was going backwards and I felt like Tony was like the older version of Qamar. I was honestly hurt to the core.

"Qort, I want you to know that I honestly care for you and during the course of the time we've been spending together I've acquired pretty strong feelings for you. I don't have these types of feelings for Diane any longer; my intentions were never to hurt you, that's the last thing I want to do to you..."

I cut him off in mid-sentence, "Tony, you're full of shit, do me a favor, turn around, drop yourself off at your girl's house and don't bother contacting me again."

"I'm not doing that Qort, we're going to go shopping in Jersey like we planned and we're going to talk about this like the adults we are."

"Tony, I have nothing to say to you, you lied to me numerous times about you not having a girlfriend, so what, was I some fresh pussy for you? You wanted to fuck me a few times before you disappeared? You know what's funny? You sit here and bark on Qamar for calling me and telling me that you want me to have him completely out of my system before we enter into a relationship but you're the one fucking me and got a whole girlfriend, did you think I would never find out? Was that what you were hoping?"

"First of all, I want to apologize to you for lying, when we first met I didn't think we would be where we are today, I didn't think we would form this friendship nor did I think I would have these strong feelings for you, I honestly thought the day we met was going to be the first and last time we saw each other, but since it wasn't and since we've been spending more and more time together I've fallen for you. If I've hurt you, I offer you my most sincere apology. I know I was messed up for lying and honestly, I did think I could get away with it; I didn't think you would ever find out about her. I'm sorry," he said but I didn't believe him, shit, for all I know he could be lying now about him being sorry.

I couldn't even bring myself to respond to him and say anything else about the situation, what I really wanted to do was beat the shit out of him but I couldn't and wouldn't, first of all I didn't want him to wreck my car trying to duck and dodge my fists and as much as I hate to admit it, I loved him and truth be told, I still wanted to continue to deal with him, that is if he wanted the same thing, if not, then so be it, men come and go.

Once we got to the parking lot of Jersey Gardens Mall Tony parked, got out of the car and came to my side to open my door, I was in the middle of texting my cousin to see if she needed anything or wanted me to get her something from the mall, she had never been so I told her to text me her sizes so if I saw something she might wear I could get it for her.

"So, you texting your new dude already?" Tony asked me.

"No, I'm texting your girl to see if she wants me to pick something up for her," I shot back while rolling my eyes at him; as much as I still wanted to be mad at him, my anger towards him was fading.

"That wasn't funny Qort, not funny at all," he responded closing the car door behind me.

"Actually it was hilarious," I told him.

On our way into the mall Tony got a call, I'm assuming it was his girl Diane, he was supposed to be at her house already, shit, I told him to call her, he didn't listen though…

Tony

I slipped the fuck up, totally slipped up, I should have taken Diane's phone call last night outside like I started to but I didn't think Qortni's shower was going to be so quick to the point that she was going to hear part of my conversation. I knew something was up last night when she put her iPod on and got to writing, I noticed she does that when she's either pissed or completely stressed. I now have to figure out what I'm going to do, what my next move is going to be, I mean Diane and I have history but I really have strong feelings for Qortni, stronger feelings than I've ever felt for Diane even though she rode my bid out with me. I have to make this right with Qortni somehow and I'm not sure yet how I'm going to do it. I really feel bad for hurting her like I did, I think I'm going to feel just as bad if not worse after I break things off with Diane, shit, as a matter of fact I was supposed to be at her crib this morning, I didn't even call to tell her I wasn't coming, I know she's going to be pissed at me, oh well, I rather be spending time with Qortni anyhow.

I expected Qortni to throw a few punches my way when I told her that I did have a girlfriend that that I had been lying to her but to my surprise she didn't, she turned the music up in the car and didn't say another word to me. I wish I knew what was going through her mind, what I would give to just be able to read her thoughts…

About ten minutes before we pulled up into the parking lot mall Qort started texting someone and me being me, I was curious as to who it was, I tried looking at her phone for a clue but to no avail, whomever it was, she was going back and forth with them for a minute. I asked her if she was texting her new dude, she told me she was texting my girl, that was a low blow, but then I thought about it, I really hoped she didn't go through my phone last night while I was sleep to get Diane's number, nah, I don't think that's her style. What's crazy is that as soon as she said that and got out of the car my phone rang and coincidently it was Diane.

"Hello?"

"Where are you at? Did you forget you were supposed to be coming over this morning?"

"No, I didn't forget, something came up, I'm in Jersey right now."

"Is everything alright with you mother? Send her my love; tell her I'll see her on Thanksgiving. Will you be coming over tonight?"

Diane was really starting to irk my nerves with all of these questions; it was like she was the damn FBI or something.

"My mother is fine, I'm not here with her, you have her number, you can send her your love and the verdict is still out on Thanksgiving dinner, I may not be coming to Jersey for Thanksgiving, listen, I gotta go, I'll let you know later whether or not I'm coming over tonight, not sure if I'm staying the night here tonight or not."

"If you're not there with your mother then who are you with? Please don't tell me that lil girl who you claim you're only friends with is who you're with."

"Not that I have to answer to you or anything but yes, she is who I'm with, she needed someone to talk to and being that I am a friend of hers I offered to drive her down here while she shops, I'm hanging up now, I'm being rude company to her."

"Don't bother calling me back or even coming over, matter of fact the things you do have over at my house will be outside tonight so you either come get them or they become street trash for anyone to take, I can't do this with you any more, I'm tired of you and your shit!" she told me and hung up in my face. I didn't even know how to react to it, I mean I have feelings for Diane, she held me down during my bid and even before I got knocked, when my brother and I used to run the streets of the Hill, he went with her twin sister Dava.

By the time I got off the phone with Diane, Qortni was already in the mall, one of her favorite stores, Cohoes, so I was on the hunt to find her.

Qortni

I was really starting to think that having Tony come with me on what was supposed to be a relaxing shopping trip was a total mistake. First he lies about not having a girlfriend, then he comes clean about some chick he's been dealing with, then when we get to the mall and are on our way in, she calls him, I had listened to enough of their conversation so I made my way into the first store I planned on visiting, Cohoes. I absolutely adored this store, it's the first store I come in each and every time I visit the mall, their clothes are very nice and their accessories are priced great, better than anything I'd find in any store in any mall in Connecticut.

I knew Tony was going to be looking for me and I really wanted to send his ass on a wild goose chase but then I remembered he had the keys to my car, so that plan was out.

I started out in the clothes section, I needed to upgrade my wardrobe badly, I picked out some clothes I thought were cute and headed to the dressing room to try them on, that's when I heard Tony calling my name, "Qort, where you at?"

"In the dressing room."

"Need help?"

"None from you."

"What's the matter? You sound like you're mad at me."

"You and all of your woman drama, you should've stayed your ass in Connecticut instead of coming with me."

"You don't really mean that, you know you enjoy my company."

I came out of the dressing room and headed to the cash register to pay for my things; Tony was right about one thing, I did enjoy his company, it was just the extra drama that came along with him that I didn't like. I really thought I had evaded the drama when Qamar and I broke up, but here I was again in the midst of more drama.

"Tony you're right, I do enjoy your company, I just don't enjoy or appreciate the drama that comes along with being in your company. It's crazy how you say you have feelings for me but, yet and still you don't respect me enough to tell me the truth about simple things, you probably wouldn't recognize the truth if it were a female with her head between your legs giving you head."

"Wow, is that how you really feel?"

"That's what I said isn't it?" I told him walking out of Cohoes trying to figure out what store I wanted to go to next. He pulled me by my arm so I would be facing him and said, "Qort, you're right, I haven't been the most honest with you. I didn't know how you would react if I told you the truth from the gate. I didn't want you to just dismiss me the moment I told you that I was dealing with someone."

"How I dealt with it wasn't for you to decide, you didn't even give me the opportunity to decide how or if I wanted to deal with you after you told me the truth. The way you handled it Tony was foul, very foul."

"I'm sorry Qortni, I really am and if you don't want to continue what we have going on any longer I can't even be mad at you, I wasn't thinking about your feelings when I was lying, I was really thinking about me and me only, do you forgive me?"

"I don't know yet, I really have to think about some things, I thought I was done with the drama and nonsense when Qamar and I broke up but it seems to have followed me and on a greater scale when we started dealing with one another, I'm not in the right head space right now to deal with this."

"I completely understand, once we get back to New Haven I'll leave you be for a while, and well you have my number and know how to get in contact with me whenever you feel like talking or being bothered by me again."

"I think that'll be for the best, I can get my thoughts together and figure out which direction I want to go in," I told him heading to the parking lot.

"Where are you going? You've only been to one store I know you're not done shopping already."

"The events of today have mentally drained me, I'm not in the mood to shop anymore, I'll come back up here next week on one of my days off. I could have gone to work today instead of putting up with this shit."

"Qortni, we drove all the way up here, you're not just going to go to one store and be done, c'mon I know you love more stores in this mall than just Cohoes."

I continued walking to my car, "Tony, I'm done shopping for the day, can you give me my keys please?"

"I'll drive you back home, I just have to make one stop to my mother's house, don't want her to find out that I was home and didn't come see her."

"Whatever, I'll stay in the car when you go visit her," I told him getting into my car.

I honestly wasn't in the mood to be bothered by Tony or any of his family, I just wanted to go home and try to sort all of this out. On one hand I could understand his plight but on the other hand he didn't have the right to try to make the decision for me, he didn't know whether or not I wanted to continue to deal with him if he told me the truth from the jump, I had a lot to think about.

We got to his mother's house and I leaned my car seat back so I didn't have to see her or make eye contact with her, I wasn't in the right frame of mind to deal with or entertain his mother today and it wasn't because I had anything against her, I didn't even know her, I just didn't want to act phony in front of her, so I leaned back and took a nap until he got back in the car.

"My mother really wanted to meet you but I told her you weren't really feeling too well so she said hopefully she'll get the chance to meet you soon."

"How nice of you to lie to her too, that must be what you're great at, lying like it's the truth. You should've told her the truth, you lied to me countless times, and that you continuously piss me off so I didn't want to be bothered by you or her, that's what you should have said to her."

I was starting to get a headache from talking to and dealing with Tony all day today. I was beyond ready to go home, take a nice hot shower and relax.

Tony

Two weeks later...

It's been two weeks since Qortni and I have spoken to one another, I've text her and called her phone but she won't respond to anything. I'm not sure if she's moved on or if she's still trying to figure things out. Two weeks ago when we got back to New Haven before bringing myself over to my brother's house I stopped by Diane's house so I could get my things and with all of the things she had to say on the phone she was acting like she didn't want me to pack up and leave with my stuff until she walked outside and saw Qortni in the car. I think she knew better than to start with Qortni though 'cause once she saw that Qort was in the car she rolled her eyes at her and I and went back into her apartment.

Qortni wasn't even trying to hear what happened with Diane and I and when I dropped myself off at Jace's house she didn't say bye or anything she just sped off. I spent the night at Jace's crib and the next morning I hopped on the train to go back to Jersey, I had no reason to be in New Haven anymore especially since Qortni wasn't speaking to me anymore.

As I was getting out of the shower I saw that a text message had come through it was from Diane, the last person I wanted to hear from and the last person I thought would be texting me.

"Hey Tony, I've been thinking a lot about you and I in the last couple of weeks and I can't get you off of my mind. We have a lot of history together and I don't want to just throw it all away, I talked to mommy the other day and she invited me to her house for Thanksgiving dinner, I told her I'd see what I can do, does she know that we're no longer together?"

I read the text a few times, grabbed my lotion and put it on and debated if I was going to answer her text or not and as soon as I was about to respond to her text, a message from Qortni came through, "Hey Tony, it's Qortni, I know you've been texting and calling me and I haven't been answering but I needed some serious me time to figure some things out. If I said I wasn't missing you I'd be lying, I miss your company, your corny jokes and just being around you. I'm pissed at you and how you've handled things with me. I thought we were better than that, but I can't and won't lie I do love you and I think there's a saying that says love conquers all, I guess what I'm trying to say is that I'm willing to give us another try if you are willing and able to keep everything a buck with me from now on."

I didn't even bother to respond; instead I called her so I could talk to her and feel her vibe through the phone.

"Hello?"

"Hello gorgeous, I got your text message."

"You know you didn't have to call me you could have simply responded by a text back."

"I know but I wanted to hear your voice and feel your vibe through the phone, I've missed you."

"You sure about that? I'm pretty sure you have a few other chicks on the side that have been keeping you company."

"Damn, all of that ma? I've been in Jersey since the day after we last saw each other and I haven't been chilling with any other females, you're the only female I'm checking for."

"HA! I've heard that line before and it was a lie 'cause you were checking for me and for that chick Diane so please spare me."

"WOW, did you really have to take it there? Just know that from now on, you're really the only female I'm checking for. Now to change the subject, Thanksgiving is a few days away, what are your plans?"

"Only thing I have planned is my brother's football game that morning other than that I'll probably just be at home, not sure if my parents have anything planned or not, my mother hasn't mentioned anything about cooking so I'm not sure, why what's up?"

"Nothing, I was just asking, I'll be here in Jersey with my daughters, mother, sisters and brothers, we try to get together for Thanksgiving every year."

"Sounds like you're trying to invite me without really asking."

"Would you like to come to Jersey to have Thanksgiving dinner with my family and I? You can finally meet my mother, my daughters and the rest of my dysfunctional family."

"Sounds like a plan, do I need to bring anything? I'm a beast when it comes to making desserts so I can bring some type of dessert with me."

"That's not necessary, you just bring yourself and everything else will be taken care of."

"I'll see you Thursday evening."

"Damn, you trying to get rid of me already?"

"No, I just have to go to work in the morning so I'm not trying to be up extra late tonight, been doing some overtime to get ready for Christmas, got shopping to do for my nephew."

"I see, well when I get up tomorrow I'll text you to see how you're doing."

"Sounds like a plan, goodnight."

"Good night sexy."

After getting off of the phone with Qortni I decided to finally text Diane back, she must have text me like three more times since I was on the phone with Qortni. Being that Qortni was coming to dinner with my family and I, I sent Diane a message saying that her coming to dinner at my mother's house wasn't going to be a good idea, first off because we're not together any longer and I needed time to decide whether or not I wanted to continue to have a relationship with her. I wasn't trying to have Qortni and Diane up at my mother's house together 'cause I know for certain Diane would have tried to get at Qortni and that wouldn't have been a good look for her, Qortni got hands, and I wasn't trying to have Diane getting her ass beat because of me.

Needless to say, Diane was pissed at me but in all reality she only had herself to blame for it because she was the one that told me to get my things from her house and that she was done with me. I mean yes, I did her dirty by messing with Qortni and having Qort drop me off at her house and lying to her telling her that Qortni was only a friend of mine, but I only did it to spare her feelings, now I need to sit and think if I really want to go back to dealing with her again and if I do, I now know to keep them far apart and not slip up again.

Qortni

I knew after Tony and I had our disagreement and everything in Jersey that I needed some time to myself. I couldn't believe that Tony had the audacity to actually drive to his girl's house with me in the car and have her come outside, I told myself to stay calm 'cause I really wasn't in the mood to be fighting her, plus per the judge I had to stay out of trouble for a year 'cause if I didn't I'd be going to Niantic for at least a year and I wasn't built for prison so I had to be on my best behavior. When I saw Tony coming out of her house with what seemed to be his belongings I chuckled to myself because not only did he manage to piss me off and get caught out by me but by the looks of things, he pissed his girl off too and she must have found out about me and told him to hit the bricks. Like dude, you're thirty-two years old and getting kicked out of your girl's crib? I couldn't even feel sorry for him because he was too old to be doing the shit he was doing.

Two weeks went by without me contacting him, answering his calls or messages, as much as I wanted to I just couldn't because I really needed the time to myself to get things in order and to figure some things out. I know y'all are reading this and probably calling me all types of dummies but you have to know that Tony was a friend before anything else, he was my listening ear when Qamar and I were together, he would come to my house and sit on my front porch with me and just listen to me vent, wipe my tears when I cried over Qamar's no good ass, this thing between the two of us goes deeper than just the great sex we have. I'm at the point with him now that if I stop all communication with him I would lose a great friend in the process and I won't lie to y'all, I kind of regret the fact that him and I crossed the friendship line and started having sex with him. Sex complicated things between us and even though he probably would never admit it I think he knows the same. Some friendships are better off staying strictly friendships, instead of crossing the line to see if things work out in a relationship because if they don't, the friendship can never go back to the way it was before.

When I did finally contact Tony I had decided that I wanted to see where this thing between the both of us was going to go. When you love someone and are in love with someone, your heart and mind may conflict on those types of decisions so you take a chance by going with one and ignoring the other; and with Tony, I decided to go with my heart, he has a hold on it and I'm not even sure he knows it. I knew Tony was going to call me after he got my message and as much as I didn't want to talk to him, hoping he would just text me back, I knew that if I didn't answer my cell phone, he'd blow up my house phone so it just made sense to just answer. I was shocked when he halfway invited me to his mother's house for Thanksgiving dinner. I really wasn't expecting it, and what I was most nervous about was meeting his mother and his daughter's. I had met his sister's before, not a big fan of them, I honestly can't stand them, but that's neither here nor there. I didn't know how his mother would take to me simply because the last time I was in Jersey I purposely didn't want to go in and see her, I wasn't in the right head space and I didn't want to say or do anything that would piss her off or make me feel uncomfortable, either way I was happy and nervous at the same time.

Thanksgiving morning...

I got up, got dressed and headed to the football field at Bowen Field, I made sure to get there early for one, because parking is always ridiculous at the Thanksgiving Day game and because I wanted to be able to see old classmates I haven't seen since maybe graduation. The Hillhouse/Cross game is the biggest rival in sports in New Haven in football and basketball, I was at the game in my blue and white and my t-shirt supporting my little brother in his last regular game of his high school career, and I was praying that Hillhouse defeated Cross if for no other reason than mere bragging rights. Thankfully the weather was absolutely beautiful, all I wore was my sweat suit with my t-shirt under it and I wasn't even cold.

Periodically during the game Tony would text me to either make sure I was still coming or just to see what the score was, he hadn't met my family yet but he was still showing support for my alma mater, I dug that a little bit, I sent him a text when the game was over, Hillhouse won seven to zip, Cross never scored. As soon as the game was over I told my family I was out and I got on the road to Jersey.

Surprisingly there was very minimal traffic driving from New Haven to Jersey, even New York was pretty quiet, I sailed through New York with no problem. When I got to Tony's house I messaged him to let him know I was outside, he came down in less than five minutes.

"Hey beautiful."

"What's up sweetie?"

"Nothing much, glad you decided to come."

"I wasn't doing anything else, my mother didn't cook, and I think my family is having Thanksgiving catered this year."

"Sounds like fun. My mother has moved since the last time you were down here; her house is like a forty-five-minute drive from here."

"Well, I think you need to drive then since you know where you're going; wait, where are your daughters?"

"I don't mind driving, they're at my mom's house already, they spent the night with her when they got here yesterday."

We were on our way to his mom's house when she called him and asked him to stop at the store and pick up a few things. Against my will he made me come into the store with him, and out of all days, I meet up with this guy I had met a few months prior when I was in Jersey, I remembered his face but couldn't remember his name to save my life.

"What's good sexy? Haven't seen you in a minute, happy holidays."

"Hey, how are you? Long time no see, happy holidays to you as well."

"What you doing around these parts? Didn't you tell me you were from New Haven?"

"Yea, I'm here visiting a friend of mine and his family for the holidays, I'm going back home tonight."

"Oh aight, well have a safe trip back, it was good seeing you!"

"Thanks! It was good seeing you too."

As soon as I finished my conversation here comes Tony, "So, who's your friend?"

"He's not a friend, I don't give that title to just anyone, he's someone I met when I was down here a few months ago."

"Yeah aight, tell me anything, he looked pretty happy to see you."

"Anyone I come in contact with is always happy to see me when they haven't seen me in a while, calm the fuck down," I was seriously getting tired of him, we're not exclusive so there's no reason for him to be playing twenty-one questions with me.

"Whatever Qortni."

"Do me a favor, have one of your family members come get you from here, I'm going back home, I didn't come all the way down here to deal with your bullshit, I can go home and chill by myself and not be stressed."

"Chill Qortni, I didn't mean to piss you off, that's the last thing I want to do, I'll drop it, I promise, I won't mention it again."

We walked to the car in silence and even drove to his mother's house in silence, I was starting to regret my decision to come down here. My patience level is like nil to none and I have a very short temper. I put my game face on when we walked into his mother's house and surprisingly I was greeted first by his two daughters, they both ran up to me and each one hugged one of my legs. Everyone that knows me knows that I love children, don't know when or if I'll have any of my own, but I love children and to see how his daughters gravitated towards me when I walked in made me feel kind of special. I wonder if he mentioned me to them prior to this week.

His mother, Mrs. Weston didn't seem too happy to meet me let alone have me in her house.

"Hello Mrs. Weston, it's nice to finally meet you," I greeted her.

"Hey," she told me rather uncouth.

I was taken aback but I swallowed it and kept it moving, I then went to speak to Tony's brothers and sisters, they greeted me with more enthusiasm than their mother.

Right before we were set to eat my cousin Amberlin called me to tell me that Qamar wanted her to give him my new number, I told her that was definitely out of the question, I changed my number because he thought it was alright to call me whenever he felt like it. Didn't he get the memo that we broke up, which meant all communication needed to cease? What part of that did he not understand? I wasn't going to let him get me all worked up, I was going to try my best to enjoy this dinner despite the fact that Mrs. Weston keeps giving me the mean look.

"Qortni, how old are you? You look a lot younger than my Tony."

Tony interjected before I could respond, "Ma, we're not doing this tonight, let's just eat dinner and watch the games, Qortni didn't come here to be asked twenty-one questions by you."

"It's cool Tony, Mrs. Weston I'm twenty-two years old."

"You do realize you're ten years younger than my baby right?"

"Is that a problem for you? It's not a problem for me and it doesn't seem to be a problem for your son. Matter of fact, wasn't Diane nine years younger than Tony? She's only a year older than me, and from what I heard, you love her, the both of you are very close."

If looks could kill I would have been dead, as this point though I didn't care, I wasn't about to have this ugly witch come for me since I didn't send for her. I'm sure Tony told her that I was coming prior to today and if he didn't, that's something she needs to take up with him, not me. If she doesn't want me in her house she needs to come right out and say something, it's nothing for me to get in my car and be out I can do without the shit today. I ain't around for it.

"Actually you're right, I am quite fond of Diane, she's been around with my son for quite some time now, she's like a daughter to me, but you on the other hand just seemed to have popped up out of nowhere, not sure what your intentions are with my son, just know I will always have my son's back," she warned me.

"Let's make one thing clear Mrs. Weston, yes I am ten years younger than Tony but age ain't nothing but a number, you don't ever have to like me, I'm not sexing you at night, I'm in bed with Tony and like I said earlier he doesn't seem to have an issue with the age difference, so I'm not sure as to why it's such a big deal to you. You can continue to have a relationship with Diane, I don't even care, and it doesn't faze me, I don't care if I never have a relationship with you, I won't lose sleep over it, please believe me," I told her getting up from the couch I was sitting on. I grabbed my coat, got the keys from Tony and was out the door before his dumb ass mother could say anything else to me. I know me and I know my temper, if she kept saying anything to me I probably would have knocked her right in her mouth and I wasn't trying to get arrested for beating up an old woman.

"Qort, don't leave, don't mind my mother, she's very overprotective of me, I'm her youngest, come on back in please."

"Nah, I'm good, I'm going home, and I have to work tomorrow so I'm peeling out early."

"Give me five minutes, I have to get the girls back home tonight, we can ride back with you if you don't mind?"

"Hurry up, if you're not out here in five minutes I'm gone," I told him looking at my watch, I wasn't playing, I was going to leave him and his daughters here if the three of them weren't back out here in five minutes.

Tony

"**M**a, why the hell you had to start with Qortni like that?"

"Because I don't trust her, I don't want her to hurt you, she looks like she has trouble written all over her."

"She's not trouble, she's not like that, she's been nothing but genuine since we've met, you gotta stop doing this to the females I decide to deal with."

"Whatever Tony, you staying here tonight with the girls? I can bring y'all to the train station in the morning."

"No, we're leaving tonight, Qort is outside waiting on us now, I have to bring the girls back tonight."

"Call me when you get in, I'll be up waiting."

"Aight ma, talk to you later."

I got my plates to go, got the girls coats on them, said our goodbyes and left, Qortni already had her car started, she looked like she was ready to bounce, I wasn't trying to get left so I made sure we were all out in less than five minutes.

I got the girls into the car, their seat belts on and got in the car, Qort still looked like she was pissed and I couldn't blame her, my mother was totally out of line for the shit she pulled.

"You've had a long day; do you want me to drive back to New Haven?"

"I don't care; I just want to get out of here as quickly as possible."

"Come get in the passenger seat, I'll drive back and I want to apologize again for how my mother acted in there, she was totally out of line."

"It's cool, I'm good just don't ever expect me to be around her again 'cause I honestly don't know what I may do to her if I'm in close proximity to her again."

"I completely understand."

I probably should have checked Qortni for basically threatening my mother in front of me and my daughters but I let it slide 'cause I know she's had a long day and I didn't want to have an argument with her and possibly have her kick us all out of her car.

Two hours after leaving my mother's house we finally made it back to New Haven, traffic in

New York was pretty backed up which set us back about half an hour. I dropped my girls off at their mother's houses and Angel tried to start some she 'cause I had Qortni around our daughter, I had to dead that and quickly 'cause I didn't want her to start with Qortni because I knew Qortni would whoop her ass.

We got halfway to my brother's house before I pulled over, there was something I needed to ask Qortni and now was the perfect time.

"Why are you pulling over? I need to get home so I can shower and get some sleep, I gotta go to work in the morning and I'm doing a double."

"There's something I need to ask you and I figured now would be the perfect time to ask you."

"I'm not sure if I'm ready to hear what you have to ask me, I can't handle too much more excitement tonight," she told me looking quite exhausted.

"You know what? Never mind, I'll wait until tomorrow to ask you, what time do you get of tomorrow?"

"Go ahead and ask me, I'm going to have this on my mind all night and all tomorrow until I see you so since you brought it up you might as well just ask me now."

"Nah, I'll wait until tomorrow, I'm going to drop myself off at Jace's house so you can go home and get ready for work."

"Whatever," she told me rolling her eyes. I now regretted that I even brought it up.

I dropped myself off at my brother's house, gave her a quick kiss on the cheek, and told her to text me when she got home.

Qortni

I couldn't believe the events of today! I should have just stayed my ass in New Haven, ate and hit the Vandome tonight; I would have been in a much better headspace than I am in now. I needed a few drinks right now with the way I'm feeling; I'm going to take my shower, have a wine cooler and take my ass to bed. I have to get mentally prepared to knock this double out at work in the morning, Christmas is coming up and I know my nephew is going to want a boatload of things and now that I'm somewhat dealing with Tony on that level I guess I have to get his daughters some things for Christmas too, maybe I'll do all of their shopping in Jersey, I can get more bang for my buck out there.

When I got in the house I grabbed my robe, and made a beeline to the bathroom so I could take my shower, my parents were still awake, watching some movie, looked interesting but I was too tired and aggravated to even try to watch it with them. When I got in the bathroom, I turned the shower on to allow the water to get hot and while I waited I sent Tony a text to let him know I made it in safely and of course I had to ask him what he wanted to talk to me about.

"I'll talk to you about it tomorrow after you get off, or I might come have lunch with you at work."

"Seriously, I want to know now it's going to be on my mind all night, give me a hint at least?"

"It's about us," was all he said for my hint, that didn't make anything better, I already knew what he wanted to ask me was about us, I guess I was going to have to wait until tomorrow.

"Okay, I'll talk to you tomorrow then," I responded to his message.

"Sleep tight beautiful, see you tomorrow."

I got in the shower, allowed the water to beat on me, a half hour later I got out, cracked open my wine cooler, took it to the head then called it a night.

The Next Morning...

I made it to work on time, actually pretty early, so I went and got some breakfast to hold me over until my first break.

"What's good Q? How was your Thanksgiving?" my boy Keon asked me.

"You don't want to know! Drama filled, aggravating, I should've stayed home and went to Vandome last night, I know it was jumpin' in there."

"Hell yea it was, surprisingly there was no drama, no cat fights, how was Tony's family with you?"

Keon and I went to high school together, he graduated a year before me, then we worked at Wal-Mart together, now we work together at the hospital, he's like my male best friend. I tell him everything, he's one of the only ones who can get me to think sanely at times.

"Man, that woman is bugged the hell out, she came at me like I was trying to throw a baby on her son, she was coming at me about the ten-year age difference between him and I and openly admitted that she would have preferred his ex Diane to have been there instead of me since she's like another daughter to her."

"She didn't say that to you, did she?"

"Hell yea she did! I told her age ain't nothing but a number and if Tony and I don't have a problem with the age difference then she shouldn't either, I'm not fuckin her at night, he's the one I'm on top of, so she needs to get over it. I left early, I couldn't deal anymore."

"Aww best friend, I know you were really looking forward to that trip, you been talking about it for a while and for it to be a disaster, I know you were pissed."

"I was plus a little shocked and just disgusted, I didn't see that coming from her, I'm not sure if the fact that the last time I was down there with him when he stopped by her house I stayed in the car because I didn't want to be bothered with either of them, had anything to do with it but whatever her problem is with me she'll have to deal with it on her own. I told him that I will never be at another family event of theirs especially if she's going to be there."

"I don't blame you, did you get a chance to meet his daughters? I know you were pretty nervous about that."

"Yeah I met them, they're adorable, they both greeted me with hugs when I walked in last night, but I have this eerie feeling that one of those girls aren't his. I didn't say anything to him about it because him and I had a little argument earlier and I just wasn't in the mood for another one, but something is telling me that the second girl he had isn't his."

"Don't say anything to him about it, that's none of your concern if she's his or not, that's something he'll have to deal with along with her mother."

"I'm not, I don't want to ruffle any feathers with either of them, she's six, I'm just hoping he was smart enough to have a paternity test done when she was born, but like you said, it's not my battle, I'm going to keep my mouth shut."

"I know it's going to be hard for you to do but I have faith in you."

"Shut up jackass."

Around eleven o'clock I got a text message from Tony, "Good morning beautiful."

"Good morning," I replied.

"How did you sleep last night?"

"I didn't sleep too well, too much on my mind."

"Understandable, I'm sorry I didn't tell you what I wanted to tell you but I knew you were tired and the way you came at me about it I thought it would be best if I told you when you weren't so tired or didn't have a lot on your mind."

"It's cool."

"You alright? I'm getting the feeling that you don't want to be bothered right now, did I do something to piss you off that I'm unaware of?"

"Nope, just the bullshit from yesterday is still heavy on my mind. Maybe we need another break from one another, I mean I see how close you are with your mother and I know you value her opinion, maybe she's right, maybe we're not good for one another or I'm not good for you."

"Stop, she's upset that Diane and I are no longer together, that's something that she's going to have to get over on her own, yes, her and Diane have acquired a relationship, one of a mother and daughter, Diane and I were together for a long time so quite naturally my mother is going to have reservations about anyone new that I start dealing with. It's just the way she is, don't pay her any mind. What time are you taking your first lunch break?"

"I only have one lunch break today, I got cancelled for second shift so I'm getting off at three-thirty instead of at eleven-thirty."

"Are you willing to come see me when you get off? I'm going back to Jersey tomorrow evening so I would love to see you today."

"I'm only coming over because I want to know what you wanted to talk to me about last night, I'm still vexed about everything that went down at your mom's house, that shit was disrespectful, embarrassing and uncalled for."

"We can talk about all of that when you get here, I'll be waiting for you."

"See you in a few."

I'm really starting to think Tony and I needed to take an extended break from one another. The things his mother said to me in front of everyone really got to me, maybe this was a sign from up above that I needed to leave Tony alone for good and not bother to look back. I just have an uneasy feeling that if we continue on its only going to go downhill from here on out.

After Work...

I didn't even bother to call Tony to tell him I was on my way over to his brother's house, sometimes the element of surprise is better than a forewarning. When I pulled up to Jace's house I saw Tony's ex-girl Diane and him outside talking and what do you know? I didn't even get upset about her being over there, I didn't even care; I shut my engine off and got out of the car only to hear Diane whining to him about how sorry she was to kick him out of her house, and how much she missed him and how she made a terrible mistake.

After about a minute of hearing her aggravating ass voice I interjected, "Sweetie, can't you see he's moved on? You had your chance, you blew it, have some dignity for yourself and just go on with your life, you act like he's the only man in the world for you."

Tony looked at me and shook his head, he knew I was going to say something, better yet, he knew I got off of work at three-thirty you would think he would have had the common sense to have her come over earlier to break the news to her so I wouldn't have seen her there with him.

"No one asked you for your opinion Qortni so please mind your damn business."

"Tony became my business the second him and I started fucking, you need to pick your face and feelings up off the floor, get into your car and drive away before things get ugly, he's told you he doesn't want to be bothered anymore, bounce! He doesn't need a weak female like you in his life, move on with your life sweetie, it was nice seeing you!"

"Is this bitch the reason you didn't invite me to dinner for Thanksgiving? Is she the reason why you won't forgive me?"

Before Tony could respond I told her, "yup, I'm the reason, the reason you spent Thanksgiving by yourself, the reason he's been too tired to fuck you when I bring him to your house early in the morning, the reason he's been staying at his brother's house every time he's in town and the reason he doesn't want to fuck with you any more, you can thank me later boo boo."

I know I can be an asshole at times and today was one of those times, and I really didn't care. After I said my piece I made my way into Jace's house and ten seconds later Tony came in behind me.

"Qort, what the fuck is your problem today? You don't even know Diane like that to have acted that way towards her."

"Does it look like I care? She was making herself look worse than she already does with all of that crying and whining, it was uncalled for, she should have taken your rejection like a G and just bounced."

"You really need to check your attitude, first the way you handled the situation with my mother last night then today with Diane, you're really on one and I'm not digging it."

"First of all, that shit with your mother last night, she deserved everything I said to her and even more that I didn't get the chance to say, she came at me totally disrespectful and I just gave her back what she put out there and as far as Diane is concerned, she's not even in my league, I was just tired of hearing her whine and cry about you telling her you didn't want to be bothered any more, like come on she was acting like she was in junior high school and her dude dismissed her, she needs to get a grip."

"You're bugged out and I think you and my mother both owe one another an apology, last night was totally uncalled for with the both of you, would you be willing to apologize to her?"

"Absolutely..."

"Great."

"When hell starts serving ice water I'll apologize. Now what did you want to talk to me about last night?"

"Nothing, I think I may have jumped the gun with what I wanted to ask you, you've been real moody and off the hook lately, what is going on with you?"

"Nothing, just tired of people thinking they can come at me any way they feel and I have to accept it, I'm just tired of everyone. I'm tired of your tired ass mother, your ex-girlfriend and I'm starting to get tired of you, I just want to be alone, I need to be by myself for a little while."

Tony grabbed me by my arm, not in a harsh way, in a sensual way, he turned me so that my back was to his chest, he began to kiss my neck while his hands caressed my body and whispered in my ear, "Are you sure you want to be alone? Are you sure you want to kick me to the curb like this?"

I was so turned on by his kisses and his hands traveling all over my body that I couldn't even answer. The next thing I knew Tony had lowered my pants just enough so he could enter my wet hot box; I was taken away by how quickly he entered me.

"You didn't answer my question, are you sure you don't want to be bothered by me for a while? I don't think either one of us can handle going without one another for a long period of time, are you sure you want to do that?"

"Yes, no, I don't know," was what I told him, his sex had me mesmerized.

As he stroked his dick in and out of my pussy he said to me, "I was going to ask you to be my one and only, let's make this thing between us exclusive."

"Okay," was the only word I managed to get out as I matched every stroke of his with a thrust of mine.

I knew what Tony was asking me and I knew what I answered him but, I wasn't sure it was the right answer. Tony and I were a couple, and I wasn't too sure how I felt about that.

"So, how do you feel about us being a couple now? We are officially off the market from anyone else," he said smiling.

"I'm not too sure how I feel about it, I mean I hope this doesn't mean that you expect me to be at family functions where your mother is going to be at because I swear to you if she comes at me like she did last night, I promise you I won't be as cordial as I was last night."

"You call how you acted last night cordial? If that was you being cordial I would really hate to see how you are when you're mad at someone. I don't like the Qortni I saw last night, that wasn't a good look for you or I."

"I was very cordial last night compared to how I normally act when someone comes at me like your mother did, she needs to be the one apologizing to me, I was merely defending myself."

"Okay Qortni, if you say so, I'm kind of tired of going back and forth with you about this situation, whatever family functions we have that my mother will be at I'll just let my family know that my girl couldn't be there because the both of you don't get along."

"Tony, I don't care what you tell your family members, just know I won't be at any of your family functions until your mother apologizes to me; I'm hungry, what are we eating tonight?"

"You've been eating a lot lately, what is going on with you?"

"Nothing is going on with me, why do you keep asking me that? I've been eating the same amount of food as I always do, sometimes I may skip breakfast or lunch so by the time I'm ready for my next meal, I'm going to eat more than I normally do."

"If you say so shorty, what do you want to eat?"

"Nothing from your mother's house I know that much, let's go out to eat, let's go to Chili's."

"Don't talk about my mother's cooking, she can cook her ass off, oh, I know what I meant to ask you last night before everything got crazy, who called you last night before we started eating?"

"Not that it's any of your business but it was my cousin Amber, apparently Qamar wanted her to give him my number, he supposedly wanted to talk to me about something."

"So you still keeping in contact with that dude? You gonna have to dead that, I'm not feeling the fact that he still wants to interact with you even though y'all ain't together anymore."

"Oh, you mean like you and Diane still interact with one another? I could have sworn she kicked you out of her crib a few weeks ago while you and I were in Jersey or am I mistaken? I don't interact with Qamar, last time I spoke to him was the day after everything went down, he called me that Friday evening and got cussed out so calm your fake Ike Turner wanna be ass down, I told her not to give him my number, I changed it for a reason."

"Keep poppin' off at the mouth, I'm gonna put something in it to shut you up. Let's go so we can eat, I'm starving and I need a drink dealing with you today."

"Whatever," I always managed to get the last word.

Tony

I swear I really thought Qortni was going to blow a fuse when she saw Diane and I outside together when she came by after work, but to my surprise she didn't. She was quite rude to Diane though and I think it was highly uncalled for, Diane was visibly upset because I told her that I wanted to date Qortni now, I mean yea, we had been through this numerous times but I always end up back with her that is until now. Qort was downright brutal with her and to her, rude was what she was to my mother last night, but she was brutal to Diane.

As soon as we got in the car to head to Chili's my phone alerts me that I have a text message and it was the worse timing ever, it was Diane texting me to see if I could stop by, Qort must've saw her name pop up 'cause she said something about it.

"So, it's alright for you to keep in contact with Diane but you were about to have a whole cow over the possibility of Qamar and I still keeping in contact with one another, if that shit isn't a double standard then I don't know what is."

"Calm down Ma, it's not even like that."

"Tell that hoe you can't stop by 'cause after you come from Chili's you'll be eating me out for dinner."

"I'm absolutely not telling her that, that's disrespectful as hell."

"Tell the hoe to stop texting you, I'm not around for that shit," I told him being serious, I don't play that oh me and my ex are friends shit, I don't trust that stuff at all.

"I'm not telling her that either, we were friends before we got into a relationship and now because you and I are together you want me to tell her to never contact me again?"

"That's exactly what I want, how would you feel if an ex of mine and I were still cool, and I'm talking cool like you and Diane, been friends for years, were in a relationship for years and then went back to being friends after we broke up, how would that make you feel?"

"I wouldn't like it but…" before I could even finish my statement she interjected.

"But nothing, if you want to remain friends with her that's cool I just won't be around and we can call this forty-five-minute relationship a wrap, better yet, fuck it, be friends with her cause I know as soon as you bring your ass back to Jersey you're going to be doing you anyhow, who am I to tell you that you can't be friends with? Do you playa."

"Why the change of heart all of a sudden? What are you up to?"

"I can't control you, I can't control who you are friends with and who you interact with, if you gonna do dirt you're going to do it, everything that is done in the dark will eventually come to the light."

She was starting to scare me, I'm not sure what she has up her sleeve but she's got me worried. I don't know whether or not she has people in Jersey near where I stay or if she has people down there that know me, either way I have to make sure I'm always on my p's and q's.

We got to the restaurant and went straight to the bar, I ordered beer and Qort ordered some type of margarita. We ate, drank, talked and just had fun enjoying each other's company, this was the Qortni that I liked being around, she was so relaxed, fun to be around and wasn't screaming my head off about my mother or Diane, maybe I needed to keep alcohol on deck for her, she was way more relaxed with alcohol in her system than she was without it.

As we were leaving the restaurant my phone rang and the number came up as private, if anyone knows me knows I don't answer private numbers. Qortni took it upon herself to answer my phone and that was a mistake on my end allowing her to do so, it was my girl Raven from Jersey, terrible timing.

Qortni put the phone on speaker, "hello?"

"Hello, may I ask who's speaking?"

"You called this phone, state your business."

"I'm looking for Tony but apparently I have the wrong number, I'm sorry for interrupting you."

"No, you have the right number, this is Tony's girl Qortni, what's your name sweetie?"

"This is Raven, Tony's girl in Jersey."

If looks could kill I would be dead no doubt, I couldn't believe this shit was happening to me today, Raven knew the drill. I would call her when I wanted to see her, she was not to call me under any circumstances, she was fucking things up for me in a major way and didn't even know it. I know all of you reading this are probably calling me every name in the book right now, let me explain something to you, I have a problem, I love women and pussy and since Qortni lives in New Haven and my official place of residence is Jersey why can't I have a girl in each state I'm in? I know I'm dead wrong for doing this to Qortni, and I wouldn't blame her if she never spoke to me again, I really need to get my shit together.

Qortni

I was dreaming? I had to be dreaming, was this shit really happening to me?! Here I was finally letting my guard down a little bit, and believing Tony had changed for the better after we had it out about him lying to me about Diane; and here he was with a whole other girlfriend in Jersey. I told him in the car on the way to the restaurant that what's done in the dark will come to light and I wasn't lying, I just didn't think it would happen so quickly.

What the hell kind of name is Raven? Who in their right mind would name their child raven, it's a damn bird and this chick Raven on the other end of this phone definitely sounded like a fuckin' bird.

"Tony, your girlfriend from Jersey is on the phone for you, would you like to take the call? It would be rude for you not to, here talk to Raven and oh, have her come get you from the restaurant since you damn sure ain't getting in my car, goodbye," I told him, I couldn't do this anymore.

"Qort, I can explain this, she's not my girlfriend, she's someone who I occasionally link up with, I haven't dealt with her since you and I started fucking, you and I both know that I spend most of my time here in Connecticut, when I do I really have the time to be with her?"

"I don't know and quite honestly I don't care, I'm tired of you and your bullshit Tony, I'm tired of you playing me for a damn fool, kiss my whole ass and please forget me and my number, I can't do this with you anymore," I told him before getting into my car and leaving him in Hamden without looking back. I had enough, first three years with Qamar with his bullshit and now Tony with his bullshit, I'm starting to think relationships aren't for me. The single life and I will be forever united; I can't do this anymore.

The tears started flooding my vision as I was driving down Dixwell Avenue and I couldn't see anymore, I had to turn into the Three Brother's Diner parking lot until I could compose myself, I couldn't believe I fell for the okie doke. He pulled the wool over my eyes again, once I started to think about how everything unfolded the tears stopped I began to laugh. I could do nothing but laugh, this dude thought he was slick. He doesn't realize that when you deal with a female, and they don't hear from you for a while, and you're not locked up or in the hospital unconscious; and they know how to contact you, no matter what agreement the two of you have with one another, she's going to find you and well as we all just saw, Raven knew how to contact Tony and got his ass caught. All I can say is that I'm happy they have one another and I hope they are both happy with one another, shit I also hope Mrs. Weston likes her, they can be one big happy family.

The next morning at work...

I couldn't wait to get to work to tell Keon what the hell went down yesterday, I wouldn't have believed this shit if it didn't happen to me.

"Qort, what's good? How did things go yesterday with you and ya boy? Did you work everything out with the situation with his mother?"

"Yo, you will not believe what the hell happened after I left work yesterday! So you know I got cancelled for second shift so instead of calling him to let him know that I was on my way to where he was at I decided to just do a pop up. You know I like the element of surprise, anyhow, I get there and who is outside talking to him? His ex-girlfriend Diane, she's out there crying and all hysterical because he told her he didn't want to work things out with her, and that he wanted to continue building with me. I got tired of watching her make a spectacle of herself so I kindly told her to basically man up and just move on."

"You and I both know you didn't say that shit kindly, I know you said a mouthful to her and probably hurt that girl's feelings," Keon told me laughing.

"I can be kind, when I feel like it and yesterday was one of those days I definitely didn't feel like being kind. Anyhow, once she leaves Tony asked me to be his girl, like the both of us exclusive with one another I told him that I was okay with the idea as long as he didn't expect me to be at any family functions where his mother will be and of course he had an attitude about that and we argued some more about the argument her and I had, long story short we go out to eat, had a great time until his phone rings and the number comes up unidentified, so me being me, I answered."

"Oh God, what the hell happened next?" he asked me laughing.

"So the chick on the other line asks me who I was and I told her that she called the phone so she needed to state her business, she says that she's Tony's girlfriend that lives in Jersey! I looked at him, handed him his phone, had some choice words with him, got in my car, and left his ass standing outside of Chili's."

"You really left dude at the restaurant? I know you went back and picked him up."

"You know me better than that, you know I left his ass right there, I told him to talk to his girlfriend 'cause if he didn't that would be rude. I'm tired of these dudes thinking they can do me dirty and I'll never find out about it, I think the single life and I are going to be best friends, I'm done dealing with dudes."

"Aww Qort, there's someone out there for you, just gotta be patient, it'll all work out for the good, you feeling alright? You look like you're pale," he told me pulling me into him for a hug.

"I'm not feeling too well, I don't know what's going on with me, I think after I finish this shift I'm going to go up to the ED to see if I can get checked out."

 "Well if you need anything let me know and text me later to let me know what the docs upstairs say after you get checked out, I'm bouncing early so just hit my jack."

"Aight homie, talk to you later."

I couldn't finish my shift, out of nowhere I began to get dizzy, started having chills and then started vomiting, one of the nurses on the floor I was working on got a wheelchair for me and wheeled me down to occupational health, I had to sign in and wait to be seen by the doctor on duty. After fifteen minutes, the doctor called my name and wheeled me to the back in a private room.

"Ms. Monroe what seems to be the problem today?"

"I'm not sure, I was fine last night, but when I woke up this morning I wasn't feeling too great."

"Any changes to your diet? Have you eaten at any new restaurants? Tried any new foods?" He asked me as he began to take my vitals.

"No to all of your questions, I've been stressed lately but I'm not sure if that has anything to do with how I've been feeling."

"Your vitals are fine, no fever, it could be stress, you may also be overworking yourself, is there any chance you could be pregnant?"

"No, well, yes but I don't think that's it," I was in all actuality hoping that wasn't the case. I don't believe in abortions and I don't want to be a single parent but with the way Tony and I have been arguing lately there's no telling what's going to happen with the both of us.

"Do you think you can leave us a urine sample? We just need enough to do a quick HCG test," the doc asked.

"Yes, I can pee for you," I told him taking the specimen cup from him.

"Would you like for me to wheel you to the bathroom or do you think you are able to walk?"

"I think I can walk there."

"Just come back into this room when you're done and I'll be back momentarily to check in on you," he told me before going to see about another patient.

"Dear God, I know I haven't been on my best behavior lately but I'm praying to you now because I need you, I don't want to be a single parent, I'm not ready to be a mother, please intervene on my behalf, and on the behalf on an innocent child who didn't ask to be born to a mother like me and a dad like Tony, in Jesus' name, Amen." I know it was probably too late to pray for a miracle, I mean if I was pregnant there wasn't anything God could do about it now, the damage had already been done. When I finished in the bathroom and went back to the room I was in, I laid down because I was starting to feel a bit dizzy, then out of no where I began vomiting like crazy, I couldn't imagine myself having to go through this for another three or four months or however long morning sickness lasted if I was indeed pregnant.

Five minutes later the doctor walked back in, my head was still over the trashcan in the room; he wet a paper towel with cold water and put it on my forehead that felt heavenly. He put gloves on so he could put the urine on the HCG test to see if I was pregnant and with each second that passed I had the eerie feeling that the test was going to come back positive.

"Your test is showing up positive Qortni but I would like to draw blood to get a good sense as to how far along you are if that's alright with you, I also want you to get an ultrasound, just to make sure there's nothing wrong with the baby," he said to me while he helped me back on the stretcher so I could lay down.

"Damn, okay, how long will it take for the results to come back from the blood test?"

"We have the results in about an hour or two but I'm sending you home for a few days to rest up and I'm writing you a prescription for Zofran, it'll help tone down the nausea and vomiting, but before you go I'll give you a dose of it now so it can help with how you're feeling."

"Thanks a mil doc, I greatly appreciate it," I told him taking my time getting off the stretcher and grabbing the prescription from him, I was taking this directly to the pharmacy down the street from my house before going home to get in my bed.

"You're welcome, someone from my office will call you this evening before we close to give you your results but in the meantime I would suggest you call your OB/GYN to schedule an appointment with them so they can start you on your prenatal vitamins and do whatever other testing or ultrasounds they need to do."

"I'll call them as soon as I get home, thank you again for everything today doc. Do I need to make a follow-up appointment with you?"

"No, there's no need, but depending on how long you stay out you may need a note from your OB saying you're cleared to come back to work."

As I walked out of the doctor's office and on my way to tell my supervisor that I was being taken out of work for a few days I remembered that Keon wanted me to text him to let him know what was going on with me.

"Hey homie, I got checked out and apparently I'm pregnant."

He replied, "You're lying, how far along are you?"

"I almost wish I were lying, I went to occupational health, they did a blood test so within the next hour or so they're supposed to be calling me to tell me how far along I am, I can't believe I'm about to be someone's mother."

"How are you feeling now? Do you need anything?"

"Nah I'm good, I'm on my way out the door to go home, they took me out of work for a few days with a prescription for the nausea and vomiting, hopefully within another few days I'll be feeling better," I sent back.

"Well if you need anything holla at me, I'm off for the rest of the week so I'll be around. Did you call or text Tony yet and tell him the news?"

"Thanks, I definitely appreciate it and no, I haven't told him yet, I'm not speaking to him right now, I need for him to explain to my why he had the balls to ask me to be his girl knowing he had another girlfriend in Jersey, as if I wouldn't have found out sooner or later."

"Qort I know you may not want to hear this right now but with you being pregnant, you may have to be the one to be the bigger person and start the line of communication, I mean he does have the right to know that you're pregnant with his child."

"I know, you're right, maybe after my nap I'll text him, he was supposed to go back to Jersey this morning, either way, he'll find out sooner or later, LOL."

"You know you're a trip and a half, I ain't fucking with you, LOL, go home, get some rest and if you need anything holla at me."

"Thanks bro," I text him back.

When I got to my car I sat in it for about ten minutes replaying the events of the past few days, I had a huge argument with Tony's mother, was pretty cruel to his ex-girlfriend Diane, found out he had a girlfriend in Jersey, I wasn't about to text or all him to tell him anything, I didn't want to be the bigger person this time and I wasn't going to be, I'd tell him when I got good and ready to and I knew it wasn't going to be any time soon, I wasn't ready to deal with his crap and damn sure didn't want to see him.

Just as I was getting comfortable in my bed at home my phone rang, it was the hospital calling me to let me know that I was about four weeks pregnant, I made a reminder in my phone to call the OB/GYN that my mother and sister go to tomorrow to make an appointment.

Tony's brother Jace and I have become close since Tony and I started going together so I decided to text him.

"Hey Jace, it's Qortni, I'm not sure if your brother is still at your crib or not but I wanted to tell you something but you have to promise me that you won't say anything to Tony."

"What's up Qort, he's back in Jersey, I picked him up from the restaurant last night and brought him to the train station, is everything alright?"

"I'm four weeks pregnant, him and I aren't on the best terms right now so I'm not telling him and I would appreciate if you didn't say anything to him as well, I'm not sure if I want to keep the baby with how things between the both of us have been."

"I totally understand, I won't say anything to him, as a matter of fact him and I had an argument last night on the way to the train station. I told him the way he's been handling himself with you is totally out of order, I told him that he needed to do better than what he's been doing. You're not like the other females he's dealt with, and I think it kind of intimidates him but that still doesn't give him the right to treat you the way he has been, meaning all the bullshit he has going on with Diane and that bird Raven," Jace replied back.

"Thank you for telling me that, I had reservations about becoming exclusive with him and went against my gut instinct, and better judgment and look at me now. I'm going to text him now and see what he says."

"Well, if you need anything let me know, I consider you family, you're my sister and you're carrying my niece or nephew."

"Thanks bro, I appreciate it."

Just as I was typing the text to Tony, there was an incoming message from him, so I read it.

"Hey Qort, I'm probably one of the last people you want to hear from and I don't blame you I just

wanted to tell you something and I know me seeing you face to face would have made it difficult and I know if I would have called you would have ignored me so I figured I would send you a text. What I'm about to tell you isn't easy for me and I really feel like shit for it, Raven isn't my girlfriend, she's someone I used to deal with when Diane and I were together. I swear to you I haven't dealt with her since you and I met, and took our friendship to the next level. She called me last night to tell me that she's pregnant, three months pregnant to be exact and I don't know what to do, she's not someone I want to have a baby by, but I can't tell her to have an abortion either because it's not my decision. I'm so sorry to have to break this to you this way but I need some time to myself to figure some things out, I hope you don't hate me for this as I didn't plan any of this."

I stared at my phone in disbelief and then started laughing, I couldn't even be mad I had to laugh to keep the tears from falling. Once I was able to compose myself I sent him a simple text then turned my phone off, the message said, "Congrats! I'm so happy for the new additions that will be coming to you and your family, because I'm four weeks pregnant by you. Take all of the time you need to get your shit together 'cause that's what I plan on doing, have a nice life sweetie!"

I laid back down and wanted to cry but the tears wouldn't fall, sometimes it's best to go with your gut instinct or if you're a woman, go along with your intuition, it almost never fails you. I knew Tony wasn't right for me to be in a relationship with, but, the sex had me hooked, his sex was on point, and it had me in a trance, so to speak. The fact that he was a friend before anything hurt, because as much as I still wanted him around I knew it would be no good. Whether it be him as a friend or as my man, when you love someone as much as I do Tony you can't be just friends with them. It's like having only half of them and everyone knows that having all of something is better than having half.

Tony

I know I should have told Qortni about Raven a while ago but was there really any point? I mean Raven and I were fuck buddies, nothing more, nothing less. Was I irresponsible when I was dealing with Raven? Absolutely which is why she's pregnant now, only question I have for her is the baby mine? Don't get me wrong, Raven is my peoples, we were friends before anything but Raven is known for getting around; having more than one prospect at a time so I'm not totally sure if they baby she's pregnant with is mine or someone else's.

I felt like a total jerk for sending Qortni the text telling her that I needed time to myself to figure some things out. I'm almost wondering if I should have told her that Raven was pregnant before knowing whether or not it's my child that she's carrying. I know my text message must have crushed her, but then again knowing her she probably looked at it and dismissed it; I wish I could turn back the hands of time with this whole ordeal Qortni and I have going on 'cause I definitely would have handled things totally different.

When I glanced back down at my phone I noticed Qortni had sent me a reply to the message I had sent her, "Congrats! I'm so happy for you and the new additions that will be coming to you and your family because, I'm four weeks pregnant by you. Take all of the time you need to get your shit together 'cause that's what I plan on doing, have a nice life sweetie!"

I definitely wasn't expecting that reply, I knew something was up with her for the past few weeks 'cause she had been eating a lot more than she normally did, her attitude was worse than it normally was, and I started having symptoms like I was the one pregnant. I must have read the message she sent to me about four or five times since she sent it to me, before I could even respond. I decided to call her because I wanted and needed to hear her voice, I knew Qortni wouldn't lie about being pregnant, I called but kept getting her voicemail so I then decided to send her a text, "Hey Qort I got your message and I want to speak with you so when you get this please call me, I tried to call you but your phone keeps going straight to voicemail, please call me back as soon as you get this message, hope to hear from you soon."

After about two hours of not hearing from Qortni I decided to call my mother, I needed some advice from her and even though she can't stand Qortni I'm hoping she can give me sound advice and put her feelings aside for my sake.

"Hey son, how are you?"

"Hey ma, I'm not too well, I messed up big time and I need some advice."

"What happened? Is everything alright?"

"No, so you know Qortni and I have been dealing with one another for some time, officially asked her to be in a committed relationship the day after Thanksgiving."

"Why would you go and do that? Now you know I can't stand her and that you're my son and I'm going to be straight forward with you but you know damn well you can't be committed to just one female at a time, you don't have it in you."

"I know ma and I was trying to give it an honest try with Qortni, it's something about her that makes me want to do better and be a better person."

"So what's the problem? If you feel that strongly about her then do it."

"I think it's too late ma, we went out to eat the other day and as we were leaving the restaurant I got a private call on my phone, I slipped up and let Qortni answer it, it was Raven on the other end and she told Qort that her and I were in a relationship, Qortni and I haven't spoken since then, I fucked up big time ma."

"Now why didn't you tie up all of your loose ends before you decided you wanted to be exclusive with that girl and when did you and Raven start back dealing with one another? I thought the both of you were done with one another when you got out this last time, and you got back with Diane? You got me all confused."

"Raven and I never got back into a relationship, she was more of a fuck buddy for me, when Diane and I were at odds I would call her up it ma, nothing more, nothing less."

"Did you explain that to Qortni?"

"She's not speaking to me ma, and besides after the message I sent her today she may not ever speak to me again."

"What the hell else have you gone and done? You just keep messing with that girl's emotions, you better watch it, remember you have two daughters and they won't be little forever. One day they're going to start dating and you better pray very hard that they don't get hurt by men the way you're out here messing with these girl's emotions."

"Raven told me the other night that she's pregnant and instead of waiting to see if the baby is mine I sent Qortni a text earlier today telling her that

Raven is pregnant and that I needed some time to myself to figure some things out."

"What was her response Tony?"

"She told me congratulations and that she was four weeks pregnant, and I know for sure that she's pregnant by me because she's been spending all of her free time with me, whether it be after work, on the days she has off she's coming here to Jersey to see me, I know she's never going to speak to me again, I tried to call her and I sent her another message but she hasn't responded to either one, I think I lost her for good ma."

"I don't even feel bad for you son, you made your bed now you have to lay in it. You knew sleeping with Raven what the possibilities were now you have two possible children on the way not too far apart, you're not working, you don't help Angel and Camdyn with your oldest daughters, how do you plan on helping these girls with these babies?"

"I don't know ma but I have to do something, especially for Qortni, I need to figure out how to get this money so Raven and I can get this DNA test done before the baby gets here because I really don't think that she's pregnant by me, I know I didn't always use condoms but I have this feeling that baby belongs to someone else."

"Well you do what you have to do and if you can come up with at least half of the money for the DNA test I'll give you the other half, one thing you don't want to happen is having to go through the entire pregnancy with that girl and she has that baby and you get attached to that baby and years down the road you find out that baby isn't yours."

"Thanks ma, I appreciate it, now can I ask a favor of you?"

"What's that son?"

"Do you mind apologizing to Qortni for everything that went down on Thanksgiving evening? She's still pretty upset about it and I think it would mean a lot to her if you apologize and sincerely meant it."

"I'll give it some thought, I won't make any promises, oh, before I let you go, you know Diane called me this morning and told me that her and Qortni had exchanged words the other day, what was that all about?"

"Nothing ma, nothing you need to worry yourself about, it's all taken care of, love you ma, I'll talk to you soon," I told her, I really wasn't trying to have to explain all of that to her, it wasn't her concern anyway, and I don't even know why Diane felt the need to call her and tell her that.

Talking to my mother put some things into perspective for me, even though she couldn't stand Qortni I knew she felt bad for her and how I handled things with her. I had to figure out a way to make things right and be there for her and our baby.

Qortni

Two months later...

Tony has been blowing my phone up for the past two months and I've ignored every call and message he's sent me; I just don't have the patience or energy to deal with him.

I was taken out of work because this pregnancy was wearing me down, I couldn't hold anything down, food nor liquid and the meds they gave me stopped working after two weeks so now I'm home on bed rest.

I got up to go use the bathroom and out of nowhere I started getting real bad cramps and blood started trickling down my legs, I already knew what this meant, I was having a miscarriage.

"God, why do you allow me to get pregnant then I end up losing my babies? It's not right, all I want to do is have my baby and be happy but apparently you have other plans for me and my life right now," I told God.

I walked back into my room to call my doctor to let them know what was going on, they told me to call 911 and the doctor on call would meet me in labor and delivery, I knew the drill all too well. While waiting to be seen when I got to L&D I sent a text to Jace and Keon, they both had been there for me from the very beginning of my pregnancy to now.

"Hey, it's Qort, just wanted to let you know that I'm at the hospital, I just had a miscarriage, don't worry about coming up here, I just wanted to let you know what was going on since you've been here for me since I first found out I was pregnant. I thank you from the bottom of my heart for all you've done for me whether it was being my listening ear or my shoulder to cry on."

Ten minutes later there was a knock on my door, it wasn't the cops this time, instead it was Keon, he was at work and when he got my message he came right up.

"Qort, you alright? What happened?"

"I'm good you know I'm used to this shit by now, I got up to go pee and all of a sudden I got hit with some mean cramps and started bleeding, I already knew what was happening, I guess it's not time for me to have children."

"Have you told Tony that you're here? Have you even seen or spoken to him since you sent him that text telling him that you were expecting?"

"No, I haven't told him, I haven't seen him either, I'm assuming he's busy in Jersey taking care of his other baby mama and child to be, he's been calling me and sending me messages but I haven't had the mental energy to deal with him and his shit, I don't want to be bothered by him right now."

"Well, let me know when they're about to discharge you, I'll bring you home, I just got paged for a discharge, luckily for me it's here in the West."

"Aight, I'll text or call your phone, thanks Keon for everything, I sincerely appreciate it," I told him; he hugged me and went back to work.

As soon as Keon left my phone rang, it was Jace, "Hello?"

"Qort, you good? What the hell happened? Have you told Tony yet? You do know he's in town right?"

"I'm alright, I was getting up to use the bathroom and all of a sudden I got real bad cramps and started bleeding, it all came out of nowhere. I haven't spoken to Tony in about two months, he's been blowing my phone up but I just don't have the energy to deal with him and his shit."

"Well him and I are supposed to be meeting up in a little while if you want I can bring him by your crib when you get out."

"Hell no, I'll deal with him in about a week or so, don't tell him I was even in he

"Aight, well if you need anything you know how to get in contact with me, I'll holla at you later to check on you."

"Thanks bro, talk to you later."

After getting checked out and my doctor doing what she needed to do I signed my discharge papers as I was walking to exit the unit I sent Keon a text telling him I was ready whenever he was.

"Meet me in the department lounge," he messaged me back.

When I got on the elevator my phone chimed letting me know I had received a message and of course it was Tony.

"Hey Qortni, I know you've received my phone calls and messages and I know you're still furious with me and I don't blame you but I really need to talk to you, I want to be there for you and our child, please text or call me back, I'm in town and I'm not leaving until we speak."

I looked at the message and decided to text him back when I got home, knowing Keon even though he didn't know Tony he would have made me text him back to see where he was and he would have dropped me off wherever Tony was, I wasn't trying to have that happen today, all I wanted to do was go home, shower, eat and go back to bed, I knew my staycation at home was coming to an end soon and I'd be back at work before I knew it.

When I got to my departments lounge I was greeted by my coworkers, hugs, well wishes, the whole nine, I was appreciative of the love they showed me. Keon came in right after me and told me he was ready, he had pulled the car up to the front of the hospital so I wouldn't have to walk all the way to the garage with him. As we walked to the car out of nowhere I started crying, it had finally hit me that I was no longer about to be a mother, my precious bundle of joy was gone, I felt like my heart was ripped right out of my chest.

"Qort, everything will be alright, trust me."

"I know I just really wanted my baby, even though I hate Tony with a passion right now, I wanted our baby to make it, it's just not fair."

"You and I both know that everything happens in God's time, when He feels you are ready to have a child it will happen."

"I hear ya, and besides, I'm still casual and I don't have any benefits so maybe right now isn't the best time to be pregnant, maybe I need to wait until I get coded for full time and benefits start to kick in, that would make more sense."

"Now you're using that big head for something, you hungry?"

"Shut up jerk and yes, I'm starving. What did you have in mind?"

"How about Chili's we can do a to-go order so you can eat and go to bed."

"Sounds good to me, call ahead so it can be ready when we get there, I want the veggie Cajun pasta, extra Cajun seasoning and a strawberry lemonade, thank you."

"Greedy ass."

We rode out to Chili's to get our food, Tony text me a few more times while I was en route home. Once I got home I decided to end the silent treatment with Tony and sent him a message.

"I guess I should feel special since you've been blowing up my phone for the past two months. What do you want from me? What other lies do you want to tell me to have me out here looking like a damn fool? I have nothing left to give you; we should have kept our relationship, as strictly friends and neither one of us would be in the shit we're in with one another."

"Qortni I never meant to hurt you and I know I've said it before but it's the truth. I should have been straight up with you from the jump about everything from the person I was dealing with on a consistent basis down to the ones I was dealing with sporadically, I'm sorry I hurt you. I'm sorry that my actions have led you to not trusting me, I want to be there for you through this pregnancy, I want to be there for our child."

"There is no more child, I had a miscarriage, so you don't have to come around anymore, you can cater to your bitch Raven and the child you're having with her."

"Qortni, call me, I didn't know, I don't want to have this conversation with you via text, I would rather have it face to face but I'll settle for over the phone."

"There's no need, I don't want or need your sympathy, I'm good, it wasn't time for me to have a child right now, everything happens for a reason, I may not know the reason but there's a reason everything happens."

"Qortni, I want us to be an us again, there's so much that has happened in the past few months when we were separated, I would like to see you so we can talk about it, please."

I think I owed it to myself to hear him out, to see what other lies he had in store for me, yes I still loved him but you know that old school song, it takes a fool to learn that love don't love nobody, Tony was only capable of loving himself and often times I wondered if he really loved himself.

"Fine Tony, we can talk tomorrow, I'm in the middle of eating and I'm not coming back out tonight."

"Thank you Qortni, I appreciate it, I really do and again I'm sorry about the miscarriage, I should have been there for you, I apologize."

"Are you done? I need to go get in the shower and work on some projects I had to put off."

"Yes, I'm finished for tonight, do you need help in the shower? I can wash your back for you, better yet, why don't you spend the night with me at Jace's house? I can cook you breakfast in the morning, we can catch up and everything."

"Goodbye Tony, I'll text you tomorrow when I'm available to meet up with you," I told him before promptly hanging up on him before he had a chance to say anything else to me.

The next day...

I woke up around ten in the morning, I was so used to rubbing my belly and talking to my unborn child,

I placed my hand on my stomach and began to cry, I missed my baby, I didn't know him or her but I missed the fact that forty-eight hours ago there was a little human being growing on the inside of me, I wondered if I would ever get that feeling back, if I would ever be able to experience having children.

I got my phone and sent Tony a text to tell him I would be there in about half an hour, the earlier and quicker I got this conversation over with him the better for the both of us so we could move on with our lives, separately. He sent a text back saying that he was at his brother's house and for me to come whenever I got ready.

Mentally and emotionally I wasn't ready for this face to face with him but I knew I couldn't keep avoiding him, this day would have had to happen sooner or later and I guess I kept postponing it until I couldn't any longer. I got up, put on some big comfortable sweats, and a sweatshirt and made my way to Tyler Street where his brother lived. When I got there I knocked on the back door.

"It's open!" someone on the other side of the door yelled out.

"I opened it and was greeted by Jace and Tony, Jace was at the stove cooking and Tony was sitting by the window smoking a bogie.

"Hey Qort, how you feeling? You didn't hit me up so I'm assuming everything is getting back to normal with you?"

"Yeah it is, I didn't want to be a nuisance to you which is why I didn't call or text you, I didn't want to be a burden to you."

"Hold up, Jace, you knew Qortni was pregnant and had a miscarriage?"

I interjected before Jace could respond, "Yes he did, I told him about the pregnancy when I first found out and when I was in the hospital I told him about the miscarriage, is there a problem? You weren't around, you were in Jersey playing house with your bitch Raven so save the dramatics for the Oscars."

"Qortni, let's go in the room and talk please 'cause this shit isn't right."

"What's not right Tony? The fact that you kept lying to me? The fact that you got caught out with another girlfriend in Jersey? Or was it the fact that you thought you were going to have your cake and eat it too, and you didn't think that all of your skeletons were going to fall out of your closet? You must not realize how fucking much I love your ass, you don't realize how hurt I was when you sent me that message and told me that she was pregnant with your baby; and here I was newly pregnant and you didn't give two flying fucks about me or our child. So please Tony, enlighten me as to what's not right."

"Qortni, me telling you that I apologize over and over again will never take away the hurt and pain I have inflicted on you. I didn't know how to handle the situation; I was scared to tell you the truth for fear of losing you. I sent you messages and called your phone for two months straight and you never once responded to them, what the fuck was I supposed to do? Come to your crib?"

"If you really cared yes, you would have gotten your ass on a train and came to my damn house if me or our child were that important to you."

I had enough of this conversation, it wasn't getting us anywhere and I was getting aggravated with him all over again, this shit was for the birds.

"You know what Tony, maybe me losing the baby was a sign that we need to just leave one another alone and move on with our lives without one another. Obviously you have things that you need to deal with before you can fully commit to someone else and I need some serious time to reevaluate my life and those who are in it."

"Qortni, I didn't ask you to come here today to argue with you, I wanted to tell you that Raven was pregnant but the baby wasn't mine. I know I dodged a major bullet with that one, I found out shortly after you started ignoring my calls and messages."

"Was that supposed to make me feel better knowing that your girl in Jersey wasn't pregnant by you? Come on Tony, let's agree to leave each other alone and hopefully forget we even knew each other in the first place. Dealing with you is more drama and aggravation than I need in my life, your mother doesn't like me, you got too many bitches in your front, back and side pockets for my liking. When you learn how to respect yourself and others then maybe we will have a chance at something but until then, I can't do it, dealing with you is draining and I don't like the feeling."

"Obviously there's nothing I can say to change your mind, I know I fucked up and I'll own that. I guess I thought the love you had for me would override the shit I put you through but, I guess I was wrong. It's crazy how you and my mother don't get along but, y'all both told me similar things that I need to do to get my shit together. Hopefully one day we will cross paths again and give this relationship thing another try, just know that my feelings for you will never go away Qortni, you'll always hold a special place in my heart."

"Very touching Tony, I'll see ya when I see ya," I told him walking out of the room. I said goodbye to Jace and left.

I can't and won't lie, leaving Tony standing there was probably one of the hardest things I had to do but

I knew for my sanity, my health and for my dignity I had to. I mean how many times are you supposed to allow one person make a fool of you? Do I love him, absolutely but, I love myself more and I have to do what's right for me. I had no business getting out of the relationship with Qamar and diving head first into bed with Tony, then trying to have a relationship with him. I didn't allow myself enough time to heal from the emotional scars I endured when I was with Qamar. I can't place all of the blame on Tony for how everything between us played out because I was a willing participant in any and everything sexual we did, I was willing to go to Jersey to have Thanksgiving dinner with his family, my woman's intuition told me he had a girl, and even though he denied it every time I mentioned it, I still decided to deal with him. So yes, as much as I don't want to place the blame or even take part of the blame for ending up where I am now, I have to. Am I going to miss him? Hell yes, as well as the ridiculous sex we used to have but I have to learn how to love myself before I can allow anyone else to love me or even attempt to love me...

August 2008...

It's been some months since Tony and I saw each other or have even spoken to one another and I miss him like crazy. The first few months were hard because he used to text me first thing in the morning and right before he went to bed at night, but, I got used to not looking forward to his messages or his calls. After the last time him and I spoke I kind of threw myself into work, I finally got a full-time position at the hospital and that position of course came with benefits so I was happy about that. My coworkers and I started hanging out with one another, we would all cook and pick someone's house to do dinner at and sometimes we would even go out after dinner, hanging with my coworkers was a great distraction for me from Tony. Sometimes I would find myself composing a text message to send to him then I would promptly delete it, I was scared that he may have moved on and had a girl in Jersey or that he was still waiting on me and didn't want to be the first one to reach out, either way, my messages never got sent.

I was sitting on my front porch one afternoon after running some errands, I had my headphones in my ears listening to some old school R&B, I was in such a zone with my music that I didn't even realize that someone had walked up on my porch, out of all people, it was Tony.

I took my headphones out of my ears and turned my iPod off, "Hey stranger, how have you been?" I asked him.

"You know, same shit different day, how about yourself? What have you been up to lately?"

"Nothing much just working, thinking about my next move, been contemplating writing a book, the verdict is still out on that one though."

"That's what's up, I see you done gained a little bit of weight, it looks good on you though. You know I haven't stopped thinking about you, about us and what could have been."

"I think I rushed into a relationship with you too quickly after breaking things off with Qamar and for that I want to apologize. I know I kept throwing the blame on you and that's not fair, I was an active participant in how everything played out too because I didn't leave when I should have."

"I'm leaving town tonight but I'll be back next week, we should do dinner, you know, catch up, nothing more nothing less, just two old friends hanging out."

"Isn't your birthday next week?"

"Yes and I would love to spend it with you."

"You sure your girl won't have a problem with the two of us hanging out?"

"Smart ass, for your information I don't have a girl, I'm single and I plan on staying that way for a long while, I have more fun when I'm not tied down."

"Cool, so what exactly do you have planned for your birthday?"

"Honestly nothing, I'm glad I saw you today, you can plan something and I'll just roll with the punches."

"Who said I wanted to hang out with you for your birthday?"

"You know you want to be around me so stop fronting, plan something and I'll be at my cousin's house next door that day so whenever you're ready to roll I'll be around."

"Whatever punk, I'll see what I can do."

"Cool, I'll see you next week then," he told me then placed a kiss on my cheek.

What did I just get myself into? I know damn well this isn't going to end well, Tony and I can't just go out to eat, he thinks he's slick. I know once we get to dinner we're going to start drinking and drinking is going to lead us to a room nearby and well we all know what's going to happen after that. Tony was the last person I slept with, and that was well over five months ago, yes other guys have tried to talk to me and some were downright bold about only wanting to fuck, but, I shot all of them down, none of them were my type, my type meaning Tony.

I knew I would have to clear my schedule for the day of and the day after Tony's birthday I know I can only speak for myself when I say this but I was well overdue when it came to sex. Tony had me spoiled; on the days I didn't have to work we would stay in the house all day and just sex each other down like we were a bunch of nymphomaniac's, I was honestly looking forward to next week with him, even if we didn't sleep together, I missed him as being my friend, I missed his presence, I missed our talks, jokes and being able to call him just to talk shit.

A week later...

"Hey jerk, I figured we could do a movie around five, then dinner and then I can bring you home...LOL," I sent a text to Tony, I wasn't trying to be out all evening with him, had work to come back home to finish up on.

"Very funny Q, movies and dinner sound good but you forgot one thing."

"I'm pretty sure I didn't but since you think I did please enlighten me, what did I forget?"

"Drinks duh! You know we can't celebrate without drinks; you must've forgot how we get down."

"No I didn't forget, when the both of us get to drinking you know where we end up and I'm not trying to go down that path again with you. We're both doing good since we've been apart there's no reason to complicate things now."

"Okay, how about this, how about we let whatever happens tonight happen, we won't try to force anything, let everything happen naturally."

I hesitated for about two minutes before responding, "Okay, I can go with that."

I showered, got dressed, made sure not to overdue it, and was on my way, as I stepped outside I was about to send Tony a text telling him to meet me at my car but luckily for me he was already outside, smoking a bogie. I swear I couldn't stand those things, but yet I smoked weed.

I got in the car and unlocked my doors, Tony finished up his bogie and said his goodbyes to his family that stayed next door, I had just finished rolling my first blunt of the night.

"I thought you quit smoking?"

"I did, just like you quit having more than one female at a time," I told him laughing.

"Ha-ha, not funny, what movie are we going to see? I don't want to see no corny shit."

"That movie Longshots just came out last week, with Ice Cube and Keke Palmer, it's looks like it's interesting, was there a different movie you had in mind?"

"No, but how about we skip the movie and go shoot pool and then we can do dinner and whatever else."

"Sounds like a plan to me, I think the only spots around here to shoot pool at are in Milford."

"What's wrong with that?"

"Our dinner reservations are in Hamden, I made them in Hamden 'cause the theater is in North Haven."

"Well, cancel the dinner reservations, we can do dinner in Milford, matter of fact isn't Outback somewhere near where we'll be shooting pool at?"

"I think so, we can do that then, it's your day old man."

"I got your old man."

We ended up at US Billboards-1 on the Post Road in Orange, he whooped my ass in pool, like five games to none, we then went to Outback Steakhouse for his dinner and it was good to reminisce with him and just catch up. The drinks seemed to be flowing nonstop and Tony and I both were getting sauced. When we got to the car Tony pinned me up against the diver's side door with his body, I knew what was coming next and I didn't fight it because a part of me was waiting for this moment to happen for a while now. He kissed me, a kiss that was more sensual and passionate than any other time he had kissed me before. He put one of his hands on my butt and I lifted my leg so it was wrapped around him, then my other leg followed, and so did his other hand, he was now holding me with his body still pressed against mine, three minutes later I broke the kiss and told him to get in the car, no other words were needed, we both knew where our next stop was going to be. I got in the car, lit my blunt and drove to the nearest hotel. When we got to the hotel, we got into the room and it was on from there. Clothes were being thrown around everywhere and neither one of us cared about where they landed, our mission seemed to be the same, sex one another down until one of us tapped out.

I don't know how many rounds we went but I know I went through five blunts and a whole bottle of Bacardi Limon mixed with Sprite. The last round is what got me though, you know how when you're so into the sex and you know beyond the shadow of a doubt that you really need to have some type of protection but the both of you are so wrapped up into one another that neither of you wants to stop to go to the store which is literally two minutes away from your hotel room to get protection so you pray to God, while your sinning because sex outside of marriage is a sin, that you don't get knocked up but you know the chances of you getting pregnant are pretty damn high? Yea well, that last load Tony nutted all in me was that nut, the nut that I knew had just connected with my egg; I said to myself, "you just got pregnant."

After the last round of sex, I lit another blunt and told Tony that I was hungry again, I think all of the sex him and I just had burned all of the food we had just consumed at the restaurant, so we went up the block to Denny's.

"I think you just got me pregnant" I told him as we were waiting to place our drink orders with the waitress.

"Don't say that Qort."

"I'm not saying that it's confirmed that I'm pregnant, I'm just saying that I think that last round was the round where you just knocked me up."

"I hope not 'because I don't want any more children, the two I have now are enough."

"Enough said," I told him as the waitress came by to take our food and drink orders.

"What's the matter?"

"Nothing, everything is good."

"You sure? You look like something is bothering you, you know I can always tell when something is bothering you."

"Nah, I'm good."

When the waitress came back with our food I asked her for a container to put mine in, I had just lost my appetite, I wasn't in the mood to eat.

"Now I know something is wrong with you, you're not eating your food and you're the one who said she was hungry, now spill it, what's the matter?"

"I said I'm good, let's not ruin tonight with an argument okay? I said I'm good so please drop it."

"Fine Qort, last thing I want to do is argue with you tonight, I don't want our reunion to end like the last conversation we had."

We sat in silence as he ate; my mind was in a million different places. I was pretty sure I was pregnant and I was pretty sure that if I was, Tony would be pissed, but here he was just months ago wanting to be there for me and our child and now he's saying that he doesn't want any more children. I guess if I am pregnant then I'll be raising my child alone. After he ate I dropped him back off at his cousin's house which was right next door to me, we rode back to New Haven in complete silence, maybe reuniting and going out tonight wasn't the best idea in the world. I had a ton of feelings bouncing around in my heart and in my head and I wasn't sure what my next step was going to be.

September 2008

I've been taking pregnancy tests for the past two weeks or so and they are all coming back positive, but yet I keep taking them hoping that one comes up negative even though one negative pregnancy test won't rule out the fifteen positive pregnancy tests that are sitting on my bathroom sink. I used to think some females were lying when they said they knew when they got pregnant, I used to think that there was no way in hell someone could know the exact moment they got pregnant but here I was five weeks after the last time Tony and I spoke and saw each other pregnant, again by him.

I stopped by my cousin Amber's house to tell her the good news, it had been a long while since her and I last spoke, she was busy in her life and I was busy in mine but I wanted her to be one of the first people I told the good news to, when I got to her house I rang the doorbell and Nathan answered the door.

"What's goodie stranger?" I asked him as I hugged him.

"Nothin much Q, what's been good with you? It's been a while since I've seen you, you been staying out of trouble?"

"Of course I've been staying out of trouble, I'm changing my ways."

"Yeah right," he responded with a smile.

"Is your woman home? Got something to talk to her about."

"Yeah, she's in the living room, I'll leave you ladies down here to talk."

"It was good seeing you Nate," I told him heading into their living room.

"Hey hoe, what brings you by?" Amber asked me.

"Oh nothing, just wanted to drop by, I have something I need to talk to you about."

"Is everything all right?" she asked me with a worried look on her face.

"Everything is fine," I told her then touched my stomach, "I'm pregnant, I think about five weeks but I won't know for sure until I go to the doctor's."

She squealed, "Congratulations boo! Wait, is it by that guy Tony?"

"Duh, who else would it be by?"

"I don't know, last time I heard a peep from you the both of you had broken up and hadn't spoken for a while."

"True, but yeah, it's his, I haven't told him yet and I'm kind of nervous to, the last time we were together he told me that he didn't want anymore children so I'm not sure how he's going to take this news."

"However he takes it just know that no matter what I'm going to have your back, now I have something to tell you."

"You and Nate went and eloped?"

"No dummy, we're expecting too, you're the first person I've told, I think Nate told Nature, I'm not too sure if he told Qamar or not, but that's neither here nor there, I'm praying I can carry this one to full term, I don't ever want to experience what I experienced before with the early birth and losing my child."

"Trust me I know exactly how you feel. I'm not going to stay too long, I just wanted to drop by to tell you my news, if y'all need anything you know I'm only a phone call away."

"I know cuz and I love you for that, and know that the same goes for you too."

Amber and I embraced in a hug, I yelled to Nate upstairs to let him know that I was leaving, and went on my merry way.

After I left my cousin's house I sent Tony a text, I didn't know if he was in town or back in Jersey, either way I needed to talk to him to tell him what was going on.

"Hey I don't know if you're in town or back in Jersey but I need to talk to you."

"Is everything alright? I'm in town, are you okay? I've been thinking about you since the last time we saw each other."

"Where are you? I need to talk to you, it's important."

"I'm in the Hill at my aunt's house."

"I'll be there in ten minutes."

When I pulled up to his aunt's house he was outside and didn't see me pull up so I beeped my horn to alert him that I was there. I killed the ignition on my car, I was starting to feel sick, I honestly didn't know how he was going to take the news that I was pregnant again, I mean according to our last conversation he didn't want any more children and here I was pregnant with what I hoped to be my first child, his third. Just as he was coming up to the driver's side door I opened it and threw up all of the food I'd ate two hours prior.

"What's the matter Qort? You alright?"

"Get in please."

"Do you feel like taking me to Elm Street so I can get something to eat?"

I started my ignition back up and he said, "I haven't been able to get you off of my mind since the last time we spoke and saw each other, the night didn't end like I wanted it to."

"I'm not sure how you wanted it to end, I'm sure you got what you wanted before it ended. Tony, remember when we went out to eat that night for the second time and I told you that I think you may have gotten me pregnant? I was right, that was the night that I got pregnant, I've taken about fifteen pregnancy tests and they all came back positive, I have an appointment with my doctor on Monday to confirm it and to see how far along I am."

"Qortni, I meant what I said that night, I don't want any more children, the two I have are enough for me, you're going to have to get rid of that baby."

That was a punch to the gut; I was absolutely not expecting him to say that to me, I wasn't sure I knew this person that was sitting in the passenger seat of my car.

"I'm not getting rid of my child, that's not an option, I don't believe in abortion."

"Well I'm telling you that I'm not around for it, you either get rid of it or get prepared to raise it yourself."

"Well I'll be raising this child myself then because I'm not getting rid of my baby. I lost one child by you already and I'm not about to purposely lose this one because we were both irresponsible yet again and didn't use protection when we slept together."

"Suit yourself Qortni."

"You are such a fuckin' asshole! I'm glad I'm able to see now how much of a jerk you really are, I honestly regret the day we reconnected, get out of my car please, I can't stomach the sight of you right now."

"I'm not getting out, I don't have my phone on me, I'm not near my aunt's house, you're going to bring me back there before I get out of anywhere."

"Tony get out of my car please or you're going to make me call the cops on you."

"Fine Qortni, I'm out and please don't bother contacting me about that baby, I don't want to be bothered and I will never be bothered with it."

"You don't do shit for the kids you have now so I'm not surprised you don't want to do anything for my child, it's nothing new, have a nice life asshole and please start putting up money for child support because I'm coming for it," I told him before driving off, I'm not even sure he was all the way out of the car before I pulled off but I'm sure I didn't give a damn either way.

Something was telling me that the real reason he didn't want to be bothered with my child was because he was dealing with someone else. Now who that person was, I don't know but I do know him well enough to know that when he all of a sudden doesn't want to be bothered he has someone he's dealing with.

I went home and cried, not the little a tear here and a tear there type of cry either, I'm talking a whole snot nose, almost hyperventilating type of cry and after about a half an hour of that I pulled myself together and realized that I needed to be strong for my child that was growing on the inside of me. Tony wasn't going to be around and he made that painfully honest. It was time for me to put my big girl panties on and do what I needed to do to prepare mentally, emotionally and physically for this baby that was coming.

Because I was hurt with how Tony handled the situation I booted up my computer and typed a letter to the last person I ever thought I'd be writing, Tony's mother, Linda Weston.

"Greetings to you Ms. Weston, I know you're probably wondering why there was an envelope addressed to you from me, I would wonder the same thing if I were you. I'm not writing to start any trouble with you and this definitely isn't an apology letter, this letter is my way of letting you know that you have another grandchild on the way. Tony and I are expecting a child sometime in late May; I know you probably won't be elated because of the fact that he's having a baby by me but we can't fight fate, it was destined to happen. I'm not expecting you to jump up and down with excitement; I'm extending the invitation for you to be apart of my child's life. Tony may or may not have told you by time this letter reaches your hands but he is not thrilled in the least bit about the child coming, he actually told me to get rid of it and that the two children that he has already are more than enough and he doesn't want any more kids but, I personally think he should have thought about that before he decided to sleep with me with no type of protection, but hey, what do I know? Anyhow, despite the fact that you and I don't get along, don't like one another, I would never deny my child's family their right to be involved in their life, hope you at least think about it, QM."

I know writing her was a bold move, I don't expect a reply from her but I know once she gets the letter and reads it she's going to tell Tony and if I said that I cared, I'd be lying my ass off.

Qortni

December 2008

The first trimester of my pregnancy was hell on earth, I wasn't prepared for all that I went through, not being able to eat or keep any fluids down, I had to have a visiting nurse come and check on me like twice a week because I was hooked up with an in home IV system, I really looked like a patient in the hospital with my IV pole and bag hanging from it. My doctors took me out of work from the end of September until the first week of December, I had something called hyperemesis gravidarum, and it's where morning sickness is heightened to the max, I was dehydrated, lost a significant amount of weight, I really thought I was going to lose this baby during my first trimester; like I did my first child in the beginning of the year but God had another agenda. My manager at work was on her bullshit, and I think it was more of a personal vendetta when she tried to get me fired by saying that I didn't have the proper paperwork from my doctor's office to be out that long. I knew the protocol, I knew what steps had to be taken in order for me to be out of work for that length of time, she was barking up the wrong tree and I told her if she got me terminated for something I did right then I would have her job and be owning that hospital. You see, my manager couldn't stand me because one of my older cousins got pregnant by a guy they were both dating at the same time, like really? When will females learn that you don't go after or get mad at the other female, you go after the guy. He's the one that was dealing with the both of you at the same time and, probably lying to the both of you telling y'all that you were the only one he was sleeping with. Women are so quick to take their frustrations out on each other while the guy sits back and laughs at their dumb asses and is laid up with the next chick. Anyway, once I got all of that nonsense squared away with her, I got paid every two weeks and out of my check I would take out at least one hundred-fifty dollars to put away for when I went on maternity leave, since I knew that I hadn't accumulated enough hours in my paid time off bank to hold me for the six weeks I would be out after having my baby. After I began the second trimester I was fine, it was like I was never sick and never experienced the all day sickness, my child thought he or she was funny putting me through all of that but, as long as he or she was healthy I would go through it a hundred more times.

Tony stood by his word and hasn't contacted me to see how me or our child is doing and I've accepted it and am prepared to raise this child by myself. Being a single parent will be rough but, I'm more than capable of doing it. When I was hospitalized last month I wanted so badly to reach out to him to tell him that I was in the hospital and if he was in town I would have appreciated that he stopped by but I knew my text would go unanswered so I decided against sending it.

When the New Year started it seemed as if Tony was a new person or one of his alter egos came out of hiding, he messaged me via Facebook on his brother's page and asked that I called him, apparently he had changed his number. I took the number down and sent him a text, only because I had the right to be an asshole to him for how he treated me since the day I told him I was pregnant.

"What can I do for you?"

"Qort, I want to apologize, I was wrong for telling you to get an abortion and that I didn't want anymore children, I had no right in doing so, I want to make things right with you and be in my child's life."

"Same song different station, you know you're beginning to sound like a broken record and I'm about tired of it. You think you can come and go out of my life as you please? That's not how it works for me and it's damn sure not going to be that way with my child, you're either going to be in their life or you're not. You're not going to treat this child like he or she is one of your bitches, you're around them when you feel like being around them."

"Qortni I know, when you told me you were pregnant I felt like you were trying to trap me, I felt like you got pregnant on purpose."

Was he serious!! This Negro had lost his ever-lasting mind and I wanted to be the one to help him get it back, no matter what it took for me to do it.

"Tony, you and I both know damn well that we were both irresponsible the last time we slept together. If I know that you don't do shit for the two children, you already have then why in God's name would I purposely get pregnant by you and trap you? If the two chicks you already have kids by couldn't keep you around with their kids why would you think I would try the same thing? I'm not the brightest bulb in the box but I'm damn sure not the dimmest either, I'm smarter than you really think or give me credit for."

"Qortni, I didn't reach out to you to argue, I reached out to you to simply ask you if you minded me being in our child's life, a simple yes or no will suffice."

"Tony, I don't care just know that I mean what I say, and I say what I mean, you will not bounce in and out of this baby's life, believe me on that."

"Can I ask you a serious question though?"

"Shoot."

"What was the purpose of you writing my mother to tell her that you were pregnant?"

"I'm pretty sure you weren't going to tell her so I decided to, I figured she needed to know that she has another grandchild on the way, you said you weren't going to be around and you didn't want to be bothered so I took it upon myself to let her know."

"Well, I'm going to be here from now on, I promise you that."

I didn't even bother sending him a response to that because I knew Tony, and I knew the next time we had a minor disagreement he would be ghost, it was only a matter of time.

The day before I was scheduled to have my ultrasound to determine the sex of my baby Tony and I had an argument over something dumb. He was adamant about coming down to come to my appointment with me and the day of the appointment he must have been on his monthly because he texts me saying that he wasn't coming, at that point I really didn't care, because it was Tony syndrome all over again. He was only thinking about himself and put himself first.

I already knew my child was going to be a girl, I guess it was the same premonition as when I knew the night I got pregnant that I was pregnant.

I think my doctor was more excited than I to find out the sex of the baby, they were so happy to see how far I had come throughout this pregnancy because during the first trimester it didn't look promising at all that I would see this day. I had a name picked out already for my daughter, never had a backup in case it was a boy, I guess you can say I was that confident in the fact that I was having a girl. When my doctor confirmed I was having a girl I could do nothing but cry, tears of joy mainly, but, there were tears of sadness as well. Here I was twenty-three years old and I had endured so much in the past three to four years of my life; I had suffered two bad miscarriages with Qamar's punk ass, and then another one with Tony. I often sat and wondered how my life would be had my other children made it. What would they look like, how would they sound? How would their personalities be? I'm sure every female that has been through something similar had the same thoughts. I had already begun buying clothes for my baby girl before I even knew she was a girl, I stuck to the neutral colors, the grays, greens, browns, yellows, I wanted something that I wouldn't have to return in the event that I was having a boy.

Mid January I began getting ready for my baby shower with the assistance of my sister and best friend, Lana. My shower was slated for the middle of March, actually on the day of Lana's birthday. I was so nervous to plan this shower, it was my first one, and I didn't know how it would turn out. I was a bit upset because none of Tony's family wanted to be involved. But it was cool, I soon got over it, my child would have the love from my side of the family. She wouldn't miss out on anything, they would be the ones missing out on a beautiful baby, they'll be the ones who'll have regrets in later in her life.

March 14, 2009

It was my baby shower day and I was nervous as hell, yesterday Tony called me while I was out running errands, I knew he was calling with some bs to tell me and I really wasn't up for it, I had about enough of him and his shit. He told me he couldn't make it in town because some family business had come up, who did he really think he was kidding? Tony must have forgotten who he was dealing with, whomever he was dealing with didn't want him to be at the shower so he made up that lame ass excuse, I didn't even trip though, I knew in the back of my mind that he wasn't going to be there so his call didn't surprise me at all.

I got up at the crack of dawn almost to get things rolling for the shower, I had to help my mother cook for the shower, I had to go get my hair done, go pick up the cake and the dinner rolls, plus I had to go to the hall where the shower was and help my sister and best friend decorate, needless to say, I was late to my own baby shower but I didn't care and my guests didn't seem to mind either.

The shower was full of so much love from family, friends, coworkers, a little bit of everyone was there and I was elated. We played games, ate until we got the itis, mingled with one another, it felt like it was a family reunion or something. When it was time to open the gifts, looking at the stage where the gifts were situated I then saw how much love people had for my daughter, that stage was full, full to the point where it took three cars and my aunt's jeep to haul all of the gifts to my house, I was so grateful to everyone. Tony never once checked to see how everything went, I was surprised but I shouldn't have been, this was common Tony behavior, and I don't think he'll ever change. Sorry to say that, but it's the truth.

After my shower I began to sort through everything, my grandmother was so shocked at the amount of gifts I received. I sat in my aunt's front room and just looked at everything that was surrounding me that belonged to my daughter, yes, they were material items but they were bought with love. I began to separate everything by size, my daughter had so many spring and summer clothes that I could change her outfit three times a day and she still wouldn't be able to wear everything she received! I knew I had to get most of her clothes separated by size because I was going to have to bring all of her things up to the third floor where I stayed at, that was a job in itself.

My sister came by one day after she got off of work to help me rearrange and organize my room to accommodate my daughter's things.

"Have you talked to Tony or has he been back up here to see you or to check on the baby?"

"He comes up at least once a week to talk to the baby but that's about it, something is going on with him and I don't know what it is, he never used to come around only at night."

"Do you know if he's involved with anyone else?"

"The way he's been acting since I told him I was pregnant it's a good chance he is, but if I ask him he'll deny it. One thing I don't think he's realized yet is that I have come to terms with the fact that he can't stay faithful to one woman and that we will never be a couple again. I honestly regret the fact that we ever introduced sex into our friendship; it complicated things and made things worse."

"Trust me I know the feeling all too well, just know that him and his family are going to be the ones losing out on a precious baby. They decided to make the decision not to be around then that's on them, they'll have to deal with that decision themselves. You don't need to stress over it, you keep doing what you've been doing to provide for my niece, and you know you have all of us here to help whenever you need it."

"Thanks sis, I greatly appreciate it," I told her before taking a seat on my bed, as time started winding down I wasn't able to be on my feet as long as I used to be.

Qortni

April 2009

I'd been on my feet all day at work and I started having contractions more frequently during my shift, which was ten in the morning until six-thirty in the evening. It was beginning to be a bit much for me so my doctor decided to take me out a month before I was due to deliver.

So, here I was a month out from having my daughter, and at home all day being bored. Tony had minimal contact with me for whatever reason, and everyone I talked to on a regular basis was still at work so I did what any pregnant woman at home all day would do, I made work for myself around the house. Being that I still had a ton of gifts at my aunt's house from the baby shower I decided that I had ample time now to get all of her gifts from the first floor to the third floor, which meant hauling things up four flights of stairs.

When I decided to take a break from moving everything, I got a random text from Tony.

"Hey Qort, I was just wondering if it's possible for Arisa to have my last name, you know my other children all have my initials."

"That's not going to happen."

"Why must you be difficult?"

"How am I being difficult? You haven't been around consistently, and now you think my child should have your last name? Yea right."

"I would really appreciate it if she had my last name, it's not that big of a deal."

"Tony, it's not going to happen, my daughter is going to have my last name, now that's the end of the conversation."

"Fine Qort, whatever you say.

Whatever he was smoking or drinking he needed to stop because there was no way in hell my daughter was going to have his last name, what would be the purpose? For him to be able to say 'oh that's my child' but still not be around for her, miss me with that bullshit please!

Tony

I know y'all hate me right now and I can't even be mad at y'all, I have a serious problem with doing people I love wrong. As I've stated before, Qortni is different from other females I've dealt with, like for instance my daughter's mothers, they do whatever I tell them to do. I told them I wanted my daughter's to have my last name and they made it happen. They didn't ask questions; they just did it. Qortni on the other hand always challenges me, if I told her to go left, she would ask why, and if I told her why she'd still go right. I wasn't used to having someone I dealt with or was dealing with challenge me like Qortni does.

Was I wrong for asking her for my daughter to have my last name? Absolutely not, that child is just as much mine as she is Qortni's and I want her to have my last name I mean she's going to have my first and middle name initials why not my last name to complete it? I really wanted to be at the baby shower with Qortni to show her family that I am going to be apart of our daughter's life, but, I had some business to handle before May gets here so I couldn't make it in town. I felt even worse when I realized that the message I thought I sent her was stuck in my draft box, it never made it to her.

I'm trying to get some things in motion so I can be in town and at Qort's side when she gives birth, that is, if she will allow me to be in the room with her. The way I've been towards her I wouldn't be surprised if she blocked me from coming to see her and the baby altogether. I need and want to do something for her that'll show her that even though we are no longer together, it doesn't mean I won't be there for our child. I owe it to her I just don't know what I can do.

I have put Qort through so much in this past year that it doesn't make any sense. I know she sometimes wishes that we never crossed the line of our friendship and slept together, I can agree that it did make things more complicated with us. I was falling for her when we were merely friends and she was still dealing with that loser Qamar. I feel terrible for how I've handled things with her but constantly apologizing doesn't mean anything to her, because I somehow always end up fucking up again only to try to apologize again.

I think my issues stem from the relationship I have with my mother and my father. My father wasn't really around for me like he needed to be leaving my mother to have to raise my and I siblings by herself and granted all of my siblings and I don't have the same father, but I think both of my parents could have made better decisions when it came to how they co-parented.

My father was and still is a lover of alcohol and my mother loved sex, so you see where I get my not so great habits? Maybe it was best that Qortni and I didn't stay together because I didn't want her seeing this side of my family, the dysfunctional side. She's never had the opportunity to meet my father and she's only been around my mother once, she's been around two of my sisters and one of my brothers, there are still a few more siblings of mine that she has yet to meet, if the opportunity ever arises.

My mother is thrilled that I'm having another child she's just not thrilled about the mother being Qortni. She said she didn't want to be bothered with the baby, especially if it meant being around Qortni. I'm really hoping she didn't mean it and once Arisa is here she'll change her mind. She should be elated that she'll have another grandchild to spoil. I'm hoping that once Arisa is born Qortni and my mother can finally put their feud to rest. It's going on almost a year since they had their falling out, and even though Qort and I aren't together any more we will be in each other's lives forever because of our daughter. I don't want my daughter to have to grow up witnessing the turmoil from both sides of her family, by the time she gets of age I want her to be able to see that even though mommy and daddy aren't together doesn't mean that we don't both love her and that she's loved by all of her family.

Qortni

Every morning, noon and night I talk to my baby girl, Arisa Logan Monroe, I tell her that her mother loves her beyond words and that as long as I have breath in my body I will do whatever it takes to make sure she has all she needs and wants. Reflecting on life I can say I am truly blessed and even though my baby girl hasn't made her grand entrance yet, I now know how it feels to love someone unconditionally. At one point in my life I didn't think it was possible for me to experience this type of love and joy, even though Tony and I aren't on the best of terms right about now, I have him to thank for this feeling for without him, I wouldn't be head over heels in love with this little person growing on the inside of me.

I still couldn't believe Tony had the balls to ask me if our daughter could have his last name, him and I weren't married, shit we weren't even in a relationship so I honestly didn't see the need for her to have his last name. Now please don't think I'm knocking anyone's decision to give their children their father's last name if you're not together, that's a personal decision, I'm not one to judge, I just know for me, it wasn't going to happen.

I can't front, I did entertain the thought, but then my father, the almighty, never holds his tongue, pastor had a mouthful and then some about me even entertaining the thought. He gave me a sermon and a half about how my daughter needed my last name because her dad and I weren't married, and then somehow he went in on me about having a child out of wedlock and how that made him feel being that he was a pastor and I'm a pastor's child. I really wasn't trying to hear any of it I mean I wasn't the first pastor's kid in history to have a child out of wedlock and I damn sure won't be the last. If he wouldn't have been so damn strict with me and kept me on a very tight leash when I was younger, I probably wouldn't have ended up pregnant. When I say he had me on a tight leash when I was growing up, I mean tight, if I wanted to go to a party while in high school he wanted to know everyone that was going to be there. Like duh, everyone that goes to the school will be there. Basketball games were another event he wanted to know the names of everyone who was going to be there, like seriously? The basketball players from both teams, the coaches and oh, the fans from both schools will be there. It's crazy to me how my dad was so quick to be upset about me being pregnant, then went behind my back and started texting people from his church to tell them that I was pregnant, like when did my business become church business? I don't deal with more than half of the people in that church because they're too damn nosy for their own good.

In my younger years I was a daddy's girl but, as I got older and when I went to high school all of that shit changed. Going into my freshman year of high school he made me purchase my own clothes, I was working for him at the church, my aunt and I would clean the church every Friday evening and I would get something like fifty dollars a week, not much but it was something. It seemed as the years passed and I got older my relationship with my father got increasingly worse to the point my junior and senior years he tried not to let me go to dances at school or even my prom but y'all know me, I always get what I want, there was no way in hell he was going to deny me the opportunity to go to my prom. That was something that I probably would have never forgiven him for if I didn't go.

I think because of my shifty relationship with my father I haven't had the best relationships with men. I don't trust too easily and I always think the next person has an ulterior motive, I have a real hard time believing people are genuine and have my best interest at heart. I swear I hope my relationships gets better as I get older, and even if Tony isn't apart of Arisa's life I will do my best to make sure my daughter knows her worth and she does a better job at choosing the men she decides to deal with, a lot better than I have done so far.

It's crazy how my relationship with my father was so strong when I was younger and my relationship with my mother wasn't the greatest and now the roles have reversed, my mother and I have grown closer since I've been pregnant and my father and I have a somewhat strained relationship, is an equal balance too much to ask for? I really don't want my daughter and future children, if I have any more, to go through the same shit I went through and am still going through with my parents.

Qortni

Time is winding down and it's getting closer to the day my baby girl will make her grand entrance. Tony messaged me telling me that his daughters were going to be performing in the Freddie Fixer parade and he wanted to see me.

"Hey Qort, my girls will be in the parade on Sunday so that means I'll be in town, if I'm not asking too much is it possible for me to see you?"

"I'll be around where the parade is, I have a cookout to go to so I don't see why not."

"Cool, I'll text you when I get in town."

"I just have one favor to ask you."

"Which is?"

"Can we sleep together? I need you to help me get Arisa out, they say sex is a good way."

"I got you ma."

Two days later…

When I got to the parade route I went straight to my friend's cookout, I was pregnant and greedy, and I never turn down free food.

I hadn't heard from Tony since he asked to see me two days ago, I'm assuming he never made it to the parade because it was nearing the end, I didn't even see his girls but then again my mind was on food so I really didn't make much effort to look for them.

Around one thirty the next morning I was in bed but couldn't sleep to save my life and I received a message from Tony,

"Hey Qort, I know it's dumb late and for that I apologize, I ran into some issues here in Jersey that prevented me from making it up there for the parade, I still want to see you if it's possible, if so I'm at the train station."

Like a pure fool I messaged him back, "I'm on my way."

When I got to the train station he was standing outside smoking a bogie, I swear I hated those things and he knew I couldn't stand the smell of them. Simple shit like that pissed me the hell off, sometimes I think he did that shit on purpose just to piss me off.

"Hey beautiful, what's up?"

"Shit, you tell me."

"I know I was supposed to come down like twelve hours ago but like I told you in the text, I ran into some issues that prevented me from making it up here. My other two baby mamas already cussed me out, so can you please spare me?"

"I don't have anything to say to you, it wasn't my child in the parade so I really don't care whether or not you made it here twelve hours ago or ten minutes ago, that's between you and them."

"So, you still want me to help you get the baby to come this week?"

"Yea, I'm tire of being pregnant, I can't do too much more of this."

"Cool, we getting a room or what?"

"Obviously, unless Angel will let us use a spare room at her house."

"Don't start Qort, that's not even funny, I'm not even going to see her, after we finish I'm going back to Jersey to handle some business."

"What is up with you all of a sudden having so much shit to handle?"

"It's nothing."

"You're lying but if you don't want to tell me then that's cool, I understand."

"You know I'm dealing with someone right?

"How would I know that? It's not like we've been on the best of terms lately, you don't tell me what's going on in your world down in Jersey."

"Well, her and I have been together for like four months now and I think it's pretty serious."

I laughed; Tony doesn't know how to be faithful to anyone but a damn cigarette and a bottle of alcohol.

"What's so funny?"

"You're funny."

"How so?"

"You think your current relationship is pretty serious yet you're in Connecticut with me, about to have sex with me; you wouldn't know serious if it handed you a million dollars.

"You'll see, I can be serious and I am serious about her and yes, I am here with you because you asked me for a favor and I can't deny my baby mother anything."

"Whatever Tony, if you say so."

We went to our all time favorite hotel, the Econo Lodge in West Haven; since we would be doing a short stay there was no reason for me to put out a bunch of money to get a room at one of the better hotels in the area that I'm accustomed to staying at.

When we got into the room it was like old times, him and I were all over each other, but it was different, the way he handled my body seemed like it was sincerer this time around. He laid me gently on the bed and kissed me like he had never kissed me before, his kisses lingered a little longer.

Right before he entered me I stopped him.

"Tony, I can't do this, we might hurt the baby."

"I'll go slow."

"I can't, you have a girlfriend, what about her?"

"Qortni, I'm with you right now, you're all that matters to me," he told me while he entered me, it hurt but felt good at the same time.

The way he sexed me that night/morning was something totally different that how I was used to getting it from him, it was like he put his all into it, it was almost like he was making love to me instead of just having sex with me.

As we made love I began to weep quietly, I didn't want him to know that I was crying. Through everything we had been through from the time I first told him my true feelings for him I still loved this man with every being in my body and it irked the shit out of me.

He rocked my body from the inside out, he had touched my soul, and it felt like he was making love to me for the first time but also for the last time.

After we finished sinning we rode to the train station in silence, my tears kept falling without him even knowing, I had a gut feeling something wasn't right with him I just couldn't put my finger on to what it was but I didn't stress over it because he was my past, granted we have a child on the way but him and I will never be and as hard as it is to convince myself that'll I'll be alright with it, I know deep down inside it hurts my heart to the core, and the fact that we just made love didn't help the situation out at all, if anything it made matters worse for me.

I dropped him off with no words exchanged between us, something was off with him an I didn't know what it was, he wasn't himself, he was hiding something from me and it must have been major.

I drove with tears racing down my face…

May 21, 2009

I have been doing the most all day today, I have been climbing four flights of stairs all day today, out of nowhere I had this burst of energy to do everything I needed to get done before my princess arrives. I have finished bringing all of her gifts to the third floor from my aunt's house on the first floor, I have managed to rearrange my room at least three more times, plus I even packed her bag and mine for the hospital. My mother told me that sometimes a burst of energy means that the baby will be coming soon and I sure hope so, even though I love being pregnant, minus the all day sickness, I'm getting a bit impatient and I'm ready to finally hold my princess in my arms.

Around six-thirty my parents were getting ready for bible study and my mother and I were joking, she said it would be hilarious if my water broke while everyone was at church, I told her it would be alright because I would drive myself to the hospital it's only a three-minute drive.

After finally finishing my room and getting all of my daughter's things in place, clothes on hangers and hung in the closet, her crib was up, sheets and cover were all ready and waiting for her.

Around eleven-thirty I finally decided to call it a night, I had been on my feet all day and my body was screaming at me to rest, I took my bath, then fixed myself a late night snack and decided to lay down and watch television. About twenty minutes after finally laying down and getting comfortable I felt something wet trickling down my legs, at first I thought I was peeing on myself but that wasn't it, my water had broken!!

I got up and waddled from the third floor to the second floor to wake my parents up to let them know, my father woke up, and when I told him he promptly went back to sleep, so that meant my mother had to do the honors of taking me to the hospital. At first I was a bit aggravated at the fact that he went back to sleep seeing how late it was but I soon brushed it off because throughout my pregnancy leading up to today he hadn't been too

thrilled with the whole ordeal of me being pregnant.
I guess I was an embarrassment to him because I
got pregnant out of wedlock. Anyhow, my mother
got up and got dressed while I was busy looking for
a pair of pants I could fit and a pad to put on to
catch the water that kept trickling out.

When I got to the hospital I went straight up to
labor and delivery triage where the nurse on duty
checked my cervix to see how far dilated I was and
to see what my doctor wanted to do with me. To say
I was nervous was an understatement, here I was a
week before my twenty-fourth birthday and I was
about be someone's mother, if I wasn't ready by
now then I knew I had to get ready and fast because
my princess was on her way. When my doctor
checked me out I was only two centimeters dilated
which meant I had another eight centimeters to go.

"Well Qortni, since you're only two centimeters
dilated you have two options, you can stay here at
the hospital and get hooked to the pitocin drip now
or you can go back home get some more sleep and
come back here at around nine. If you decide to stay

here now and get things going you won't be able to eat any solid foods until after you have the baby."

"I'll come back, I'll be able to sleep, get my hospital bag, shower and eat before I come back, I can't see myself doing too well without eating for a long period of time."

My mother told me she would be waiting for me downstairs, she was going to have the valet bring her car since we were going back home.

"Well, Dr. Evans will be on call when you get back, you're familiar with her right?"

"Yes, I know all of you in the office, I wanted to get to know all of you so by the time it was ready to deliver everyone would be well versed on me."

"Good thinking, I wish all of our patients thought the way you did. Before I let you go I just want to be the first to congratulate on the birth of your daughter, I know you are going to be a great mother to her!"

"Aww, thank you Dr. Stevens, I truly appreciate it and I appreciate all that you and the rest of the staff have done for me and my daughter so that I could see this day come to fruition."

"It was my pleasure, I know you didn't want to go through anything else tragic so we had to do what we had to do in order for this child to be alright and come into the world, now go home and get some rest, be back here around nine so you can get things moving so you can finally meet your baby girl!"

When I got back home I changed the sheets on my bed and put towels under them to absorb the water from when my water broke. After changing the sheets, I sent Tony a message to let him know that today was the day that my baby girl Arisa would be born.

He text me back, "What time will you be going back to the hospital?"

"They told me to be back by nine."

"I'll be there."

"Okay."

After I woke back up I sent a message to my sister who was ironically in nursing school during her OB rotation and told her that I was on my way to the hospital because my water broke, she told her instructor that she needed to leave and she met me at the house, her, my mother and I all went to the hospital together.

When I got back to the hospital I was taken into one of the birthing rooms, I told to undress and put on the hospital gown, which I did, then my doctor and nurse came in and hooked me up to the fetal monitor, the pitocin drip to get my contractions to start so I could dilate quicker and a monitor to keep track of my contractions oh and I can't forget the IV they had me hooked up to and all I could think about was the fact that sometime today I would be a mother; my life wasn't about just me anymore, my world now revolved around my daughter Arisa.

Around six in the evening I was still pregnant, the contractions were coming a bit closer together but they were nothing I couldn't handle, my mother, sister and I were all talking, cracking jokes, this labor was easy going so far, except for the fact that Tony had yet to show up.

"Hey, I'm not sure where you are but my doctor said I should be having the baby within the next two hours or so, are you close by?"

Instead of sending me a text to reply he called me.

"Hello."

"Hey Qort, I'm not going to be able to make it into town tonight, something came up and I have to take care of it, I'm sorry ma."

"You're absolutely right, you are sorry and so am I, I'm sorry I ever gave you the opportunity to come back into my life, you can take all of your sorry's and shove them up your ass," I shouted at him through the phone and quickly hung up on him.

Two and a half hours later...

At eight-fifty in the evening on May 21, 2009 I gave birth to my beautiful baby girl Arisa Logan Monroe, she weighed six pounds, five and a half ounces and she was twenty inches long, she was perfect as far as I was concerned.

My sister and my mother really came through for me, the last forty-five minutes of my labor were the absolute worse, but thankfully my sister helped me through the tough contractions and my mother kept talking to me to help me keep my mind off of the pain. They both stayed with me until I was brought up to my room, they went and visited my baby girl in the nursery and then left, they had work and school in the morning so for the rest of the evening it was me and my baby girl hanging with one another.

Occasionally some of my coworkers that worked second or third shift would stop by, they wanted to see 'their' baby, most of my coworkers were so elated when I told them I was pregnant.

Arisa woke up every two hours religiously to eat, I breastfed so my nurse would wake me up every two hours when she bought Arisa in to eat, after the first two feedings I decided to stay awake 'cause I sure wasn't going to be able to get any rest at the rate I was going, the hospital staff was constantly in and out of my room either to bring Arisa in to eat, to do my vital signs or to see how much I was peeing and to see how I was feeling, I swear the hospital is the last place to try to get sleep in.

The Next Day...

I began getting visitors in as soon as the sun came up it seemed like and I didn't mind. I got up at the crack of dawn because I couldn't sleep, so I then decided to see if my nurse could remove my IV so I could take my shower; I began to smell myself and it wasn't a pleasant scent at all, I needed to fix that and fast.

Tony hadn't called to check on Arisa or I and I took it as the beginning of him showing and proving that he wasn't going to be around for us, more so for Arisa. It was cool though because I wasn't going to let anything or anyone take my joy away from me, my daughter was going to know that I had her back no matter what.

Mid-afternoon shifting into the early evening hours Tony sent me a message saying that he was on his way. My parents were visiting with me, not too much conversation going on with us, but they were there nonetheless. Tony and my parents had never had the pleasure of meeting one another, my brothers had seen him a few times and weren't too fond of him and I couldn't blame them. I was really hoping my parents were gone by the time he got there, I didn't want any unnecessary drama to pop off in my room.

My father saw Tony as he was entering my room and alerted me that I had a visitor coming in, when he got in the room my father was holding Arisa. Tony gave me the balloon and teddy bear he purchased for my daughter, washed his hands and I introduced everyone to each other. Shortly after my parents left, my father handed my daughter to Tony and told me he'd be back tomorrow to pick me up when I was ready to be discharged.

Tony held our daughter and tried to make small talk with me.

"She's beautiful Qort."
"I know she's my child."

"Correction, she's our child."

"You can claim her when you start helping me with her."

"I didn't come up here to argue with you, I came to see you and the baby. How was your labor?"

"Fine."

"Were there any complications?"

"Nope."

"Am I bothering you with these questions?"

"No, your presence is bothering me, when are you leaving?"

"Qort, one minute you want me around and when I am around you want me gone, what's the problem?"

"You and your inconsistency is my problem, you're around when it's convenient for you but when it comes to anyone else but Tony, you don't have time for it, Tony only gives a damn about Tony. But Tony doesn't realize that it's not about him anymore, it's about the children he has now from the oldest to the youngest."

I regret the day I told him that he could be in the life of my daughter; Tony was a part-time dad with his daughters so me having a child by him wasn't going to change him. I think he finally realized that he wasn't able to control and talk to me the same way he does his other baby mothers; I'm cut from a totally different cloth than he was used to.

"Qortni, there is so much that I want to tell you and probably need to tell you but I don't want to hurt you any more than I have done already. I feel like all I've been doing lately is hurting you and it's not my intent and it's certainly not being done on purpose."

"Tony, it's cool, honestly with how you've handled situations with me in the past I'm sure I don't have any feelings left, I'm pretty sure they have disappeared because I'm so used to being hurt, not too much can hurt me unless it's the loss of a loved one."

He took a deep breath, handed me my baby girl, kissed me on my forehead and said, "I'll see you later Qort, heading back to Jersey tonight."

"Let me guess, something important you have to handle right? It's always something more important than those who should be your first priority, which are your children. Goodbye Tony."

"Goodbye's are for those you won't ever see again."

"I know; goodbye Tony."

Tony had an awful way of getting me to think about things I didn't really want my mind on. What could he have possibly told me that would have hurt my feelings? Did his mother die? God forgive me but that wouldn't have hurt my feelings, I probably would have been relieved because I wouldn't have to deal with her anymore. I racked my brain for all of half an hour to try and figure out what he wanted to tell me and when I kept coming up with nothing solid I stopped trying to figure it out, I had a brand new bundle of perfection that needed all of my energy and focus.

For the remainder of the evening Arisa and I ate and watched our favorite basketball team, the Lakers, play until we drifted off to sleep.

Qortni

June 2009

It hasn't even been a whole month since I gave birth to my daughter, and already I'm feeling like I'm getting back to my old self. Tony hasn't been around, he hasn't even offered to buy pampers or formula for our daughter, it was aggravating to say the least but it was also expected from him. I called him one evening to see if he was in town and told him that I need a case of pampers for my daughter, he said okay. An hour later his nephew rings my doorbell and in hand has a case of pampers; now I really didn't need the pampers because one of my coworkers who works on the floor my room was on hooked me up with two black trash bags full of pampers; I really only asked just to see if he was going to come thru for my daughter.

I had been wanting a new tattoo for some time now and I decided to get my daughter's name tatted on my back. I called Arisa's Godfather, Kalil to see if he could watch her while I went to get tatted. When I got to Kalil's house, his friend Wassim was on the phone with him, he told Kalil to give him my number.

"Yo, my boy Wassim wants your number, is it cool for me to give it to him?"

"Yeah, it's cool, I don't mind, I remember big head."

Kalil gave Wassim my number and he text me to tell me to lock his number in.

I told him I was on my way to get a new tattoo and that I would text him as soon as my tatt was complete. I was surprised at myself for even agreeing to give Wassim my number, in my heart, I still belonged to Tony but since it looked like he wasn't interested in giving me the time of day anymore, I figured, what the hell, it's time for mommy to get back in the game, and the fact that Wassim didn't seem to mind the fact that I had a new baby at home was a plus; rumor had it that he's had a crush on me for a while.

Qortni

July 1, 2009

My baby girl has been such a blessing to me, she has changed me for the better, my attitude has changed tremendously and I just feel better. Tony hasn't been around to see her and I'm alright with that, he's the one who is missing out on a beautiful baby girl and when she's older and looks back on pictures and sees that it's only her and me in them he'll have to be the one to tell her why he wasn't around.

I started back to work on the first of the month, it was bittersweet, I wasn't ready to leave my baby girl after being with her for six weeks, but I know I needed to work so I could make money to spoil her with.

My first day back was hell to say the least; as soon as I walked into my departments lounge who the fuck do you think was amongst the first people I saw sitting in the lounge? No one but Qamar; I don't know what trick was being played on me but I wasn't laughing. Qamar was the LAST person I wanted to see or be working with.

"What's up Qortni? Congrats on your baby, how have you been? You're looking good as usual and the baby weight you put on looks good on you."

I looked at him and simply stuck my middle finger up at him. I didn't want to have a conversation with him. Did he really expect me to? I went to my manager and told him that Qamar and I couldn't be around each other and that he needed to stay off of my floor and far away from me, we did have restraining order against one another but I wasn't sure if they were valid at our place of employment.

I was very uneasy because Qamar was now working at the same hospital as me and in the same department, I felt like I wanted to quit but I knew that wasn't an option; I just prayed that he kept his distance and nothing popped off between us.

Later that afternoon...

My day was going by pretty quickly, work was going smoothly, I was on a new floor with better hours, the staff seemed pretty cool; I was on my way to the building that was connected to the building that I worked in, I hadn't had the time to make my rounds to see all of my coworkers since I came back to work. As I was just about to walk onto the unit my girl Nic worked on when Qamar came out of nowhere and pinned me to the wall.

"Listen Qortni, I don't know what the fuck your problem is with me but I'll be damned if you talk to me like you did this morning in the lounge."

"Qamar, get the fuck off of me! Have you lost your ever-lasting mind? Did you not learn anything from the last time you put your hands on me? Do you need a reminder?" I couldn't believe he had the audacity to put his hands on me again! This fool was really bugged out and I was sure he needed some mental help.

"Qort, I'm sorry. Seeing you this morning in the lounge made me realize how much I've missed you and when you didn't speak to me I felt some type of way. You seem so much happier now, and I want to make you happy like that again."

"Again? Qamar, you never made me happy, you caused me more pain and grief than I'd like to remember. I'm only going to ask you this one time, please stay the fuck away from me at work and outside of work or I'll be forced to have a restraining order put against you while we're at work. Take heed to this warning before things get ugly for you," I told him before walking onto the unit to see my old coworkers.

I couldn't believe him! I couldn't believe he had the balls to put his hands on me yet again! I guess the ass whooping I put on him over a year and change ago wasn't enough. Make no mistake about it, yes I have a brand new baby at home but please believe if his punk ass gets it twisted again I will revert back to my days before I had my daughter and whoop his ass again for him.

I visited my girl Nic and my other former coworkers on that floor for about fifteen minutes, I went back to my floor to do my last rounds so I could leave early, I was off for the next three days and I planned on enjoying them with my baby girl.

Qortni

July 4, 2009

It was Arisa's second official holiday, the first being Memorial Day; I dressed her up in her Fourth of July outfit that I picked up on one of our many mommy/daughter shopping trips. I had been invited to a few different cookouts so once I got Arisa's diaper bag packed with enough diapers, change of clothes, bottles and formula, my baby girl and I were out.

As I was on my way out the door I was greeted on my front porch by one of Tony's sister's, Leann, a very unpleasant surprise. I don't do well with uninvited guests just popping up at my house, that was a no-no.

"Hey Qortni, were you on your way out? I wanted to come by and visit Arisa, you don't mind do you?'

"Actually we are on our way out and I do mind because you didn't call first, I don't take kindly to people just popping up at my house. I'll let you come in this time but please don't make a habit of just coming by my house unannounced, it's quite rude," I told her rolling my eyes.

"I do apologize but since Tony told me you lived right next door to our cousin and I saw your car still here I figured I'd come by."

"You always show up to peoples houses unannounced?"

"I wasn't sure if you were going to come by later so I decided to stop by just in case you didn't show up; do you mind if I hold her?"

As I was about to hand Arisa to her Aunt Leann, she began to cry, I'm a firm believer in babies and kids sensing when people aren't genuine. I put Arisa over my shoulder to calm her down and once she calmed a bit I tried to hand her to her aunt again and again she began to cry.

"I don't think she's comfortable with you, she only cries when people who aren't real want to hold her. You weren't sure if I'd show up where later?"

She reached to try to take my daughter out of my arms, "Let me see her," she told me while ignoring my last question.

I smacked her hand away and told her, "Did you not hear a word I just said? I just told you I don't think she's comfortable around you, babies can sense things adults can't always pick up on, step back please," I told her as nicely as possible because I really wanted to smack the piss out of her.

"Okay, well I guess I'll be going and maybe I'll see you later at the cookout," she told me heading to the door to go outside.

"If I see you, I see you if not then oh well," I had really had enough of Tony's family, they were all bugged out and what cookout was she talking about?

As I was pulling up to one of my cousin's houses I got a text message from Casper the ghost himself.

"Hey Qort, it's Tony, my family is having our annual Fourth of July/family reunion at East Rock park, I'm extending an invitation to you for you and Arisa to come through, I haven't seen either of you since the day after she was born and some of my family members want to see the baby."

Here he goes with his bullshit and like an idiot I responded that I would come through. Here he was only inviting my daughter and I to the cookout so he could show my daughter off, and act like he's the fucking daddy of the year, he had his family fooled but he damn sure didn't have me fooled. I spent an hour or so at my cousin's gathering before I made my way over to East Rock Park.

When I got close to the park I asked him what end of the park he was at, he told me closer to Cross High School so I parked in the parking lot adjacent to the school, got my daughter and her diaper bag and made my way across to the park. Tony greeted me as soon as I ascended the stairs.

"Thank you for coming, it means a lot to me."

"Anything for you so your family doesn't think you're a deadbeat dad," I told him snidely.

"Can we not do the whole back and forth thing today? Please? I have my daughter's here with me, I'm just trying to enjoy my family with no drama."

"I make no promises, you asked me to come here so you can show my daughter off as if you've been in her life since she's been born and this is only the second time you saw her," I told him as we sat on some benches away from the rest of his family.

He took Arisa from me and started playing with her so I took my phone out and started reading some of my emails.

"How have you been?" he asked me.

"Let's not do the small talk, go ahead spend some time with my daughter so I can be out, I have other places to go before it gets late."

"How about you go ahead and leave the baby here with me, you can come back when you're done."

"That's never going to happen, when I leave my daughter leaves with me."

"Qortni, she isn't my first child, I've been taking care of children for a long time now."

"Really? Which ones? Definitely not your two children."

When he put his left hand up to wipe the sweat from his head and adjusted his fitted, that's when I saw it, on his ring finger; I grabbed his hand, "What's that?"

"It's a wedding band," he told me, avoiding eye contact with me.

"So, when did that happen?"

"May 23."

"Wait, that was two days after I had Arisa, that's why you were in such a hurry to get back to Jersey the evening you came to see the baby?"

"Yeah. Qortni I wanted to tell you but I didn't know how to tell you, I didn't know how to tell you without hurting you for the millionth time."

I was speechless, my heart was bruised, I was shocked, not really mad, more surprised.

"Congrats."

"That's all you have to say?"

"What else do you want me to say Tony? I hope your marriage doesn't last? I hope you don't treat her the same way you've treated your past relationships? What, you want me to say what you already know to be true that you jumped into this too quickly? Let me ask you this, how does she feel about the fact that your daughter was born two days before you and her got married?"

"She doesn't know about Arisa; she knows about my other two daughters but she doesn't know about the baby."

I laughed, "how long do you plan on keeping it away from her? She's going to find out sooner or later."

"I don't know; I haven't figured out how to tell her yet but I will."

I grabbed my daughter's diaper bag then took her from him, I was leaving, I didn't have anything else to say to him, I wanted to inflict bodily harm on him but that wouldn't end too well plus I had my daughter, so I couldn't resort to my old way of resolving issues.

"Where are you going? You've only been here for a little while and my family hasn't had the opportunity to see the baby."

"I'm leaving Tony, it was a mistake for me to come here and right about now I don't really care if your family ever meets my daughter," I told him as I turned and started to descend down the stairs.

"Qortni please don't go, we can talk about this, please just hear me out, please?"

"Nah I'm good, good luck with everything."

Tony

Back in New Jersey

I knew I couldn't hide my marriage from Qortni forever but I didn't want her to find out like this. I felt like shit because I know the feelings Qortni possessed for me and I know how I feel about her. Never in a million years did I think I would end up married, but here I am.

My wife and I have known each other for just a short time but when you know it's right you make your move then. It was so hard and it hurt so much knowing that I couldn't tell Qortni the real reason I couldn't make it to the baby shower or to the hospital when she was in labor, my wife kept getting suspicious when I kept leaving to go out of town when I was going to visit Qortni and have my one on one time with Arisa when Qort was still pregnant with her, I had to cut my visits to CT down because my wife was starting to ask questions and believe it or not I didn't want to keep lying to her.

I know I won't be able to keep Arisa from my wife forever I just have to find the right time to tell her.

"Baby, you look like you have something on your mind, is everything all right?" my wife Talia asked me.

"There's something I need to tell you but I'm not too sure how you're going to take it."

"What do you need to tell me Tony?"

"Come sit down."

She sat across from me, "I'm sitting now, what's the matter?

"Remember how before we got married I would make frequent trips to Connecticut late at night? I wasn't going to see my brother, I was actually going to see my youngest child's mother, I would sit in the car with her and rub her belly and talk to our daughter."

"Your daughter? I thought you only had two children?"

"I had a baby girl two day before we got married, which is why I had to go to Connecticut the day before our wedding so my baby mother wouldn't trip, she had already cussed me out for missing the birth of our daughter. I knew if I went to Connecticut and stayed for a few days you would start to get suspicious."

"Why didn't you tell me about her sooner?"

"I didn't want to tell you before because I was afraid of losing you, I didn't know how you

would react to it."

"So why did you decide to tell me now?"

"Because it's been eating me up inside knowing that I've been keeping this away from you, I knew I wasn't going to be able to keep it from you forever, I'm sorry."

"So, who's her mother?"

"Her name is Qortni, we used to date but there were some issues that kept us from continuing our relationship."

"Okay, this is a lot to process but I'm glad you told me and didn't continue to keep it from me."

"I'm hoping Qort and I can come to some type of agreement to get Arisa here for the weekends so she can interact with us, I want to form a bond with her, she's my baby girl."

"The next holiday is Thanksgiving and we'll be in New Haven so how about seeing if she'll be willing to allow the baby to come spend the evening with us, it's worth a try."

"That's why I love you, you always got my back and never judge me."

"We have to have each other's back baby; marriage is about compromise."

I didn't honestly think Talia would be as understanding as she was, I began to wonder if she was being too understanding, I don't know of any female who would be fine with knowing that her new husband had a brand new baby that was born just two days before they got married; I guess that's what makes Talia one of a kind.

I already knew Qortni wasn't going to agree with Arisa staying with me and my family for Thanksgiving, especially with my wife being there, I was going to have to try to work something out with her.

Qortni

Tony was married, he had a real ring on his finger, he had a wife, he was off the market. He hurt me, he betrayed my trust, to say I was crushed by the news would be a total understatement. As much as I tried to convince myself that I wasn't still in love with Tony, I knew I was lying to myself.

Now all of his "something came up" moments finally made sense to me, he was preparing for his wedding that whole time. My heart felt like it was ripped right out of my body, I should have been numb to all of the hurt and pain I had endured over the past few years from Qamar and Tony, but hearing Tony admit that he was married was a totally different type of hurt and pain.

I started to wonder what his wife had that I didn't that made him choose her over me to be his bride. He knew damn well how I felt about him and it felt as if he just said "fuck Qortni's feelings," and went about his business. I can tell you one thing though,

I'll be damned if he thinks my daughter will be anywhere near his wife, I want to meet her before my daughter is ever in her presence; I'll be damned if that bitch tries to inflict any harm on my daughter because she's feeling some type of way about Tony having a baby who is two days older than their marriage.

Qortni

August 2009

Tony and I haven't been on the best of terms lately, he hasn't been around to see Arisa, he hasn't been helping out financially, he's been doing absolutely nothing and it's starting to really piss me off, he just doesn't care. The last time I talked to him was a few weeks ago, I needed him to come with me to the Department of Social Services so we could fill out the papers for child support. After almost a month of procrastinating on taking his portion of the paternity test, he finally did, so now we had to do the paperwork.

On my one day off from work I was spending it on Bassett Street at the Social Services building, not something I was looking forward to. Being that it was crowded in the building I decided to bring Arisa outside to get some fresh air since Tony hadn't even showed up yet. As I was playing with Arisa outside this guy that went to high school with my older brother happened to be walking up Bassett towards me, I think we noticed one another at the same time.

"Qort, long time no see, how have you been?"

"I've been good Markus, how have you been? How long have you been in town?"

"I just got in town night before last, you know I only stay for a short time, nothing but trouble here for me. Is this your little mama?"

"Yes, this is my baby girl Arisa," I told him while turning Arisa around so he could see her face.

"She's beautiful Qort, just like her mother," Markus told me with a wink.

Back in the day I had a major crush on Markus, he played basketball with my oldest brother when they were in high school, it was something about him that stood out to me more than the other guys.

"Thank you sweetie, well, her dad just pulled up, we gotta go in here and handle some stuff for your little lady."

"No doubt, get lil mama right. Give me your number so we can stay in contact, I can't believe you're all grown up now with a baby of your own."

"Yeah I ain't little no more," I told him laughing. We exchanged numbers and he went on his merry way.

"Who the fuck was that Qort? All in your face and in my daughter's face, what the hell is up with that?"

"None of your damn business as to who that was, your business should be your wife, you remember her right? The chick you married two days after my daughter was born, now can we go handle our business please?"

"Why must she be so damn difficult? Aren't you glad I never acted like that towards you?" Tony's baby mother Camdyn asked him. I guess she thought I didn't hear her but I did, loud and clear.

"Listen bitch, what Tony and I discuss is between him and I, what the fuck are you doing here anyway? Last time I checked Tony didn't need a chaperone here with him to sign paperwork.

"I got your bitch, you young, insecure piece of shit."

Tony interjected, "Can we not do this today please? Like seriously, all of this isn't even necessary, y'all are acting real fucking childish and it's uncalled for."

I told him, "Tell that thirsty, dusty baby mama of yours to learn how to mind her business."

"Bitch you 'bout to make me run you a fair one, keep coming out of your mouth sideways towards me."

"Name the time and place shorty, you ain't saying nothing but a fuckin' word."

Tony shook his head and said, "Camdyn, you can leave now, I just needed a ride here and I specifically asked you not to start with Qortni today and you just couldn't keep your damn comments to yourself. You always trying to start some shit and it's not necessary."

"Fine Tony, have it your way, don't bother coming back over to the house after you finish with her," Camdyn replied as she rolled her eyes and walked off.

"Why would you even bring that bird with you?"

"Qort, please don't start. I asked her for a ride down here, that's all, I didn't even want her to get out of the car but she insisted, she said she wanted to see the baby."

"Whatever Tony, can we go in so we can get this stuff done today so I can go about my business, please?"

"Have it your way Qortni. You know, I was thinking, you know my birthday is coming up, how about you, me and Arisa go out to eat or something? I haven't really spent too much time with her."

"You just realized you haven't spent enough time with your daughter? I don't mind doing lunch afterward, you're paying though."

"How you gonna make me pay for my birthday lunch? And to answer your question, no, I didn't just realize I haven't been spending enough time with her, I've been realized it, I just don't want to be bothered with your smart-ass mouth every time I come to town to see her. We're going to have to come to some type of common ground when it comes to me spending time with my daughter. You know your family doesn't like me, so coming to your house to see her is out of the question."

"If you really wanted to see her, despite how my family feels about you, you would make an honest effort to see her, liker seriously, enough with the excuses, I'm tired of hearing them."

"We'll work something out and soon."

We handled our business with Social Services and went out to lunch. I can't even front on y'all, it felt damn good being in Tony's presence again, regardless of how much we argue, disagree or stop talking to one another for any length of time, we always come back a little stronger. Being out to eat with him and our daughter soothed my heart, even if it was temporary; I knew sooner rather than later he would return to Jersey to be with his wife.

"So, have you told your wife about Arisa yet or is it still the elephant in the room at your house?"

"I told her, she wants me to see if it's possible for you to let Arisa come with me and my family to Thanksgiving Dinner this year, we'll be in Connecticut at my sister's house, my sister you met on my dad's side."

"Tony, you know that's not going to happen unless I meet your wife first, in person, one on one."

"Why do you need to meet her in person first, do you not trust her?"

"Honestly? I don't trust either one of you, and I don't trust your family and you know I don't like half of them anyway."

"It's not fair to keep my child away from her family on my side, she needs to get to know my side of the family Qort."

"It's not fair how they outcast her before she was even born, now either I meet your wife prior to

Thanksgiving or my child spending the holidays with you is a no go, simple and plain."

"I'm telling you now, you're not going to meet Talia, that's never going to happen so get that out of your head now. You do know I can take you to court to get partial custody of Arisa right?"

"You know that in the state of Connecticut you are considered a deadbeat dad because you left me during the pregnancy right? So your chances of getting any type of custody of my child is nil to none, but please, by all means, try and go for it, I have all of your messages saved and ready to print out when you were cussing me out, telling me my child isn't yours and all of the derogatory things you said to me while I was pregnant with Arisa."

"Have it your way Qortni, I just want to be in my daughter's life, that's all, I don't want to keep arguing with you, I don't want to go weeks or months without seeing her, I just want to get to know her and have her get to know her father, am I asking for too much?"

"No, you're not asking too much but you have to realize something Tony, you haven't been the easiest person to get along with during my pregnancy, I don't fully trust you anymore, and you're going to have to prove to me why I should trust you again. You have hurt me time and time again and I haven't fully gotten over it. You think you can just walk out of my life and back in whenever you feel like it, it doesn't work like that; it's not fair to me or my child."

"I hear you Qort and for all the times I've hurt you, I do apologize, I just want to do right by Arisa, be there for you and her, that's all I want."

"Actions speak louder than words."

We ate our lunch and I rode around just so Tony could spend more time with Arisa. At times I felt as if I was too hard on Tony but then I would think about all of the broken promises he made me and made our daughter. When I was pregnant with Arisa, Tony would drive down at night to have his daddy/daughter time with her, he would talk to her, rub my belly and even bring me food at times; I wished those times would last forever.

There's no doubt that I love Tony, mainly because he gave me my first child but I'm still in love with him as well, you can't help who your heart falls in love with...

Tony

I couldn't believe the way Camdyn acted with Qortni, she was totally out of line, all she was supposed to be doing was dropping me off at Social Services and bouncing, I don't even know why she thought it was necessary to get out of the car. I know she mentioned to me something about seeing my daughter but I think she just really wanted to start some shit with Qortni, but she really didn't know what she was getting herself into by starting with Qortni. I was really secretly praying that they didn't come to blows because Camdyn can't fight for shit and Qortni got some hands on her. There have been times when Qortni and I would play fight and even though she's small in frame, Qortni got hands for days.

I just wanted to come, handle my business with Qortni so we could get this paperwork done so Qortni and I could get this paternity test done and over with. I haven't been helping her financially like I should be and I have no one to blame for that but myself.

Being around Qortni and our daughter was good for me, and not to mention that the baby weight Qortni had looked good on her, I promised myself to behave though, I am a married mad now. I really didn't expect Qort to agree to go to lunch with me for my birthday, I knew for my actual birthday I would be in Jersey with my wife, but for some reason, I felt the need and urge to spend some quality time with Qortni.

I still love Qortni and still have very strong feelings for her, I know I'm married but the truth is the truth, it's not easy to just turn off feelings for someone you've been with and have known for some time.

I wasn't surprised that Qortni shot down my suggestion for Arisa to spend Thanksgiving with my family, especially for the simple fact that she's never met Talia. I won't lie, I don't want them to meet because I'm scared of what Qortni may say to Talia, I'm not trying to have no shit pop off between the both of them, cause then I'll be forced to choose and I would undoubtedly choose my child over my wife; hopefully as the time passes by and Qort sees that I am making a real effort at being in our daughter's life she'll be more open to me having Arisa with me for Thanksgiving, I mean our daughter should know both sides of her family...

About the Author

Rocky Rose was born and raised in New Haven, CT. **Rocky** began to perfect her writing style and seriously value her ability her sophomore year in high school. Only after her English teacher noticed and expressed to Rocky how much talent Rocky had did she begin to believe. Rocky's story, which was read by many of her friends in high school, proved that her imagination was phenomenal, and that she could create wonderful images and scenarios in her mind first, then on paper. Writing was not only fun for Rocky; it also served as an outlet for her emotions. She never had the type of relationship with her parents where she could talk to them about anything so she wrote down her feelings instead. Even though writing came naturally to her, Rocky never once thought about pursuing a writing career until 2005 when she enrolled into the *Breaking Into Print* writing program, where she completed the course and received her diploma in just two years.

In November of 2010, Rocky met her mentor and sister, Karen E. Quinones Miller, who told Rocky that she had *raw* talent. Rocky began writing her first novel, *My Man My Abuser*, which is about three years of her life in which she was in a domestically violent relationship. In 2012 Rocky co-wrote *I Win You Lose*, which is a compilation of six short stories dealing with Domestic Violence.

Rocky Rose

When Rocky isn't writing she enjoys spending time with her daughter and son, going bowling, to the movies and shooting pool. Rocky resides in New Haven, CT with her daughter and son.

Coming soon from Author Rocky Rose...

I Win You Lose 2 will take you on the journey of new characters who are abused physically, mentally, emotionally and verbally. Are you ready?

Bruised Never Broken Qortni is back in the last part of the My Man My Abuser trilogy. After suffering a major heartbreak with

Tony, Qortni vows to never love again because love, to her, only leads to heartbreak. A couple of months after having her daughter Qortni finds herself dealing with a few different guys, trying to rid herself of thoughts and feelings of Tony, which only leads to her hurting herself even more. Qortni goes on a sexin' spree where she sleeps with guys and leaves the money on the table for them. After a couple of years of doing this, Qortni meets this guy who she thinks is the one to rid her of her feelings for Tony and her abusing her body sexually. Will this new guy be who Qortni needs her to be or will be break her heart like Tony has done?

The first erotic novella, Initiation is about two brothers who are ready to pledge their frat's elite division. Their marriages, family dynamics and lives are put to the test. I hope you're ready for the sexiness that Salt is about to bring your way!

Pastors Kyd takes you through the life of Adira Simpson who despises being the child of a pastor and minister. Adira shares with you the ups and downs of being the child of a pastor. Is Adira the next in line to be called to the ministry?

Lost Faith…Have you ever dealt with a situation where you couldn't see the light at the end of the tunnel? Have you ever been angry at God for a situation you were dealing with or going through? Join me in my journey as I uncover thoughts, feelings, and how one major situation changed my life and how I lost all faith in God and eventually regained it.

Books you should check out....

*My Man My Abuser introduces* you to nineteen-year-old Qortni Monroe is the daughter of a well-known pastor from New Haven, CT. She meets twenty-year-old Qamar Daniels and soon after they meet the form a relationship. Qortni doesn't find out until six months into the relationship that Qamar is Satan himself, and she's scared to death that if she tries to leave him he'll to kill her.

Qamar is a twenty-year-old no job having leech. He meets and falls head over heels in love with Qortni but the feelings are definitely not mutual. Qamar has a huge self-esteem issue which causes most of the arguments and fights between him and Qortni.

Will Qortni stay in the relationship until Qamar kills her? Or will she have sense enough to leave him and spare her life?

I Win You Lose takes you through the lives of characters who deal with different types of Domestic Violence, physical, mental, emotional and verbal. You will cry and feel heartfelt sympathy for the characters in this book. I Win You Lose was co-written by Rocky Rose and L. Marie, both of CT.

In life you have to put a STOP to anything that is causing you pain, you have to let it go. You have to make peace with your past to have a successful future. Colleen Williams did just that in her book, STOP. She poured her heart out by writing letters to her abusers letting them know all the pain they have caused her. It's Colleen's time to STOP and share her story with you.

The meek, Ruthie Belle dreams of one day being free from her husband's constant mental and physical torment, until one day she finds the courage to break free from his bondage. Even though the plan goes without a hitch, Ruthie spends the rest of her life riddled in guilt and shame. Later at the ripe age of 103, Ruthie discovers forgiveness and redemption are a part of everyday journeys.

Excerpts from Rocky's stories in I Win You Lose Psycho

My girls and I decided to hit up Club NV and I'm so glad we did 'cause the shit was definitely jumping that night. As soon as we got to the club we had guys buying our drinks and I wasn't arguing. I started off with a mimosa then followed up with two Amaretto Sours, and after my second one I was definitely feeling a buzz. Guys were pulling me to dance with them in every direction possible and I didn't turn any of them down. Shit, with the outfit I had on, why wouldn't I want to be seen on the dance floor?

As I was dancing with this fine man who was donning white linen pants, a white linen shirt and white AFO's, someone came from out of nowhere and grabbed me almost causing me to lose my balance and bust my ass. I couldn't immediately tell who it was, but once we got up under some light I was pissed, it was Jaylen. What the hell did he think he was doing?

"You think you can just disrespect me like that and get away with it?" Jaylen asked me while tightly holding onto my left arm.

"Disrespect you? Have you lost your fuckin' mind? We are not a couple we just met! You need to let my arm go before you get your ass hurt," I told him.

"Bitch, you must think I'm playing, I'm so fuckin' serious; is he the reason you didn't want to tell me where you and your girls were going tonight so you could come dance with ol' boy over there? You definitely got me fucked up, you belong to me and if I'm not around, then you don't dance with anyone, do you understand me?"

Of course me being me, I started laughing, laughing so hard I started crying, "Jaylen, sweetie, you have some serious issues, we just met earlier today and now you're acting like we're a couple; what did I tell you earlier today? I'm not around for the bullshit, I don't do drama, and you are to never put your motherfucking hands on me because doing that is as good as signing your own death certificate. Now I'm going to ask you nicely to take your hand off of me before shit gets real ugly."

Do you know this fool had the audacity to haul off and smack me right in the club? I couldn't believe it, and I think me biting his hand, kneeing him in his balls and knocking him the fuck out caught him totally off guard, shit, I surprised myself. Did I not tell this joker earlier today that I didn't do the drama, bullshit or him putting his hands on me? I could have sworn I gave him fair warning, and he still had the audacity to come up in here and put his hands on me, and had the nerve to tell me I was disrespecting him? He had officially brought out the bitch out in me, and I hate bringing her out.

Light At The End of The Tunnel...

I kept blinking my eyes trying to bring my surroundings into focus, the last thing I remembered was Jason holding me up by my neck choking me and throwing me against the brick wall in my kitchen. I was finally able to focus in on where I was, and as soon as my vision came in focus, excruciating pain in my right arm suddenly hit me like a ton of bricks, I yelled because the pain was almost unbearable.

"Ms. Wright, are you alright? We're glad to see you're back with us. You've been out of it for about three hours. Do you know where you are and why you're here?" This medium height, light-skinned female asked me. Looking at her she seemed to be in her early twenties, slim build, with real pretty micro braids and her badge said that her name was Eryka Brown.

"No, I'm not alright, my right arm is hurting tremendously. Can I get something for the pain please? I know I'm at the hospital and the last thing I remember is my boyfriend and I arguing, him choking me and throwing me up against the brick wall in my kitchen. Who brought me in here?"

"I will tell your nurse that you need something for the pain. Is there anything else that I can get for you? A gentleman by the name of Kendall brought you in here; he said he's your neighbor. You are very lucky to have someone like him as a neighbor, had it not been for him getting you here when he did, you could have slipped into a coma."

"I'll have to thank him when I see him again. Do you mind turning the light off or at least dimming it, the brightness is making my head hurt more. Do you by any chance know when I'll be able to go home?"

"I'll can turn them off, and if you'd like, I can close the door as well. The doctor's will probably want to keep you for a day or two just for observations, just to make sure you don't slip into a coma and to monitor your vital signs. I'll send your nurse in so he can answer any other questions you may have."

"Thank you, Eryka, I really appreciate it."

"No problem at all."

After Eryka left my room, I tried to drift off back to sleep but as soon as I had gotten comfortable, there was a knock at my door and my neighbor Kendall Jackson peeked around the door.

"Hey you, how are you feeling?"

"I'm in a lot of pain, but had it not been for you I would be a lot worse; I appreciate what you did for me. How did you know what happened to me?"

"I saw when ya man had left, and that you didn't walk to the door with him like you normally do. When I didn't see you at the door, I noticed his shirt had splotches of blood on it, so when he pulled off I came to your house and saw you weren't responding to my calls, so I called the ambulance. "

"I really appreciate it and I owe you big time."

Before Kendall could respond, there was another knock on my door it was my nurse. Kendall told me that he would see me later and left. My nurse asked me a series of questions and told me I would be staying at the hospital for two days. They could monitor my vitals so I wouldn't slip into a coma. Once I finished talking to my nurse my doctor came in and did his overview of me, and asked me some very personal questions about how I ended up in this predicament, and I did my best to give him one word answers to all of his questions because I didn't want him all in my personal business. I would handle this matter like I did every other time, by myself.

I finally made it to my room and no sooner than I arrived I was greeted by the last person I wanted to see at that moment, Jason, and this fool had the nerve to be holding a teddy bear that said 'Get Well Soon' and a bouquet of flowers, the nerve of him.

"Jason, what the hell are you doin' here? I don't want you in my room, don't want you anywhere near me, now can you please excuse yourself?"

"Maya, I know you don't mean that, your meds are making you say all of that. You know why I'm here; I'm here to help my woman get better. I came to see how you were doing and I came to bring these to you, you know, to cheer you up a little bit," he told me while trying to hand me the teddy bear and flowers.

"Jason, are you hearing yourself? You threw me into a fuckin' brick wall! You tried to kill me earlier today, and now you're saying you're here trying to help me get better, to cheer me up? You can get the hell out of here and out of my life for good to help me get better and to cheer me up," I told him while reaching for my nurse call button.

"Yes Ms. Wright, can I help you? Is everything all right, are you in any pain?" asked Tanya, my nurse.

"No, no physical pain. Only pain I'm experiencing is this asshole here in my room. Can you please have security escort him out? And I want him to be placed on a Visitor Restricted List please. Can you make that happen Tanya?" I asked while lookin' at Jason the whole time, letting him know how serious I was about not wanting to be bothered with him anymore.

"Yes, I can make that happen. Let me call security and have them come up and handle this situation for you. Do you need anything else?"

"No, that will be all for now, thank you."

I guess Jason thought I was joking because after Tanya left he had the nerve to make himself comfortable on the couch that was situated under my big window in my room.

"Jason, did you not hear when I asked you to leave? Did you think I was joking? I would really appreciate you leaving my room and my life and never returning, this nonsense between us needs to stop and I'm putting a stop to it now," I told him.

Before I could blink my eyes a good three times he had my right arm twisted back behind me and my head in a headlock. I screamed at the top of my lungs with tears pouring out of my eyes because this crazy bastard had officially lost his God-given mind. The whole nursing staff on my unit rushed into my room and pried Jason off of me. When the cops arrested him, I glimpsed over at him and I swear I saw hell in his eyes. Tanya asked me if I wanted to press charges and I told her yes, the first time in the three and a half years I was pressing charges on the one man I thought I loved.

Bye Baby

"Good morning love, how did you sleep last night?"

"I slept ok." She replied short and curt.

"I didn't sleep too well, our argument last night just kept replaying in my head and I think you took what I said the wrong way. You know I love you and I didn't want to make it seem as if I was saying that had you gotten pregnant by anyone else they wouldn't make an honest woman out of you. I was just saying that there a lot of guys out here that would just allow you to be their baby mother and that's about it. Throw a couple of stacks your way, fuck you when they feel like it and keep doing them when they're not around you, and you know that's not my style, so I'm going to do the right thing and make you my bride. I'm not worried about the counseling sessions, we can go to the justice of the peace if you'd like, I just want to make you happy babe."

"I don't recall asking you how you slept last night, 'cause quite frankly I don't give a damn, but I do hear and understand what you're saying Kegan. And I do

313

appreciate you for stepping up to the plate and taking care of your responsibilities. You are a real man, and those are hard to come by, and believe me, I do consider myself the lucky one just on the strength that you put up with me." She replied with a little smile.

I pulled her in for a big hug. She may irk my nerves at times, but it's no secret that she has my heart.

"Babe, how about I tell my job I won't be in today, and I accompany you to your appointment? I would love to see what our child looks like and hear its heartbeat."

"No, you go ahead to work. I'll call you with the results. You need to go ahead and make that money."

I started to tell her that I was going with her anyway but I decided against it, I wasn't trying to have another argument with her this morning. I didn't have the energy for all of that and I didn't want to stress Acasia out.

"Fine Acasia, call me as soon as you have your results, and we'll do something to celebrate tonight if the results come back positive."

"Alright love, I'll call you in a couple of hours to let you know what the doctor says. I'm about to hop in the shower, care to join me?"

"Of course I'll join you. When have I ever turned down an opportunity to bathe with you?"

After we made love in the shower we both got dressed and headed our separate ways.

~Three Hours Later~

I can't even concentrate at work 'cause my mind is wondering how Acasia's appointment went and if we're going to be parents. I'm as anxious as a kid the night before Christmas. I've never been this anxious for anything before. I was just about to call her when she sent a text that read, "Congratulations, you're going to be a father!"

I called her as soon as I composed myself, "babe, we're really going to be parents? No bullshit!"

"Yes baby, we're about to be parents! I can't believe I'm about to be a mother. I'm scared babe—I don't think I'm ready for this." She replied, her voice becoming faint.

"Nonsense baby, we're going to be great parents. You have a big heart and a lot of love to give. There is no doubt in my mind that you will be a great mother. How about I cheer you up and we go shopping for your ring today? I'm going to leave work early, meet me at the house so I can pick you up and we can go get your ring."

"Are you serious, we're going to pick my ring out today? Baby I love you! I'm on my way to the house now. I'll see you when you get there."

I hung up the phone with Acasia, went and told my boss the great news, and told him I needed to leave early so I could go celebrate with my boo, he gave me the O.K. but not before telling me that he and his boss had thought it over and decided to give me the promotion we had talked about earlier that week.

When I got to the house Acasia was sitting on our front porch waiting for me.

"I see you're all ready to go, didn't feel like waiting in the house for me?"

"Nope, you coming in the house would have been wasting too much time, so I just decided to wait right here for you. Are you ready or do you need to go into the house for anything?"

"Nah, I'm ready now. I have some good news as well, nothing that tops your news of the day, but something pretty close."

"What's your news baby?"

"I got that promotion at my job, my supervisor told me right after I told him our good news. I start next week as the Chief Editor for the company. I get my own office, personal assistant, and of course more money, which will definitely come in handy now that we have a little person on the way. How far along did the doctor say you were?"

"That's great baby! I'm so proud of you! My husband to be is making major moves! I'm two months pregnant. In another three months we'll be able to tell what the sex of the baby is, matter of fact, while we're out, we should start looking at cribs, car seats, and strollers, never too early to start looking right?"

"It's still early, but if you'd like to look then we can go window shopping today. Anything to make my wife happy," I replied while leaning over to kiss her.

When we made it to Michael's Jewelers, Acasia almost broke her neck running over to the engagement ring case.

"Is there anything I can help you with this afternoon?" asked the sales associate.

"Yes, I'm looking for my dream wedding ring set. I want something that pops, but not too large, and I want the sparkle to be big." Acasia replied with the biggest smile on her face.

"Okay, what's your preference? White gold, yellow gold, or platinum?"

"I love both platinum and yellow gold, to me white gold is just platinum that costs less."

"What is the budget looking like?" the sales associate asked looking at me.

"My max is ten thousand, nothing too good for my future wife."

"I'm sorry, I didn't even introduce myself, my name is Camille Jackson, and I will be glad to help you choose the ring that best fits your heart's desire."

"Nice to meet you Camille, my name is Acasia and this is my fiancée Kegan."

"Now, did you want a diamond engagement ring or a gemstone engagement ring?"

"Diamond ring, I have enough jewelry with emeralds."

As the two ladies discussed rings I went over to the section where they had the jewelry for men. I made a mental note to come back here in a couple of weeks so I could treat myself to a couple of new pieces. I saw a couple of rings that I was digging, a couple of bracelets that I was definitely liking, and a pair of diamond earrings that I told another sales associate to hold for me, I was going to come back tomorrow to get those. Acasia called for me to come back over to where she and Camille were. They said she had found her dream ring.

"What kind of ring is that? It's definitely shining and it's a nice size, I like it." I asked Camille.

"This right here is a Halo Diamond ring set in platinum, asking price is only two thousand dollars; the great thing about shopping here at Michael's Jewelers is that you won't see anyone else with jewelry like yours. We have one of a kind jewelry."

"That is great; babe, does this ring make your heart smile? Is this the one you want?"

"Yes, it is, I absolutely love it; I was thinking about going with yellow gold, but I absolutely love this ring. This is definitely the one, Kegan."

To order or pre-order any books by Author Rocky Rose please send an email to authorrockyr@gmail.com with *Book Order* in the subject line or you can go directly to her website which is http://www.booksbyrocky.wordpress.com/

www.ingramcontent.com/pod-product-compliance
Lightning Source LLC
Chambersburg PA
CBHW070218260626
47160CB00002B/591